PRAISE FOR THE LEGEND OF SENSEI TSINELAS

"*The Legend of Sensei Tsinelas* is a beautifully poignant tale of a young boy's journey through grief and self-discovery. Jason Tanamor captures the struggles of Victor Dela Cruz, who—in the face of bullying and loss—must learn to embrace his Filipino heritage and identity. Tanamor deftly tackles the complexities of mental health and the courage it takes to confront our darkest moments. With a touch of superhero flair, his storytelling delivers a powerful punch, highlighting the resilience of the human spirit and the inner strength every young hero must discover within themselves."

—Robin Alvarez
Author of *When Oceans Rise*

"*The Legend of Sensei Tsinelas* is an authentic exploration of cultural identity and what it means to be a young Filipino American in today's world. Jason Tanamor deftly juxtaposes seventeen-year-old Victor's superhero fantasies with the reality of his daily life to highlight his emotional struggles after his parents' sudden death. This is an entertaining and important read for today's youth that tackles more than just cultural identity but also self-acceptance. It is refreshing to read genuine Filipino community representation in these pages."

—K. M. Levis
Author of *The Girl Between Two Worlds* (Engkantasia series)

THE LEGEND OF SENSEI TSINELAS

THE LEGEND OF SENSEI TSINELAS

JASON TANAMOR

Ooligan Press | Portland, Oregon

The Legend of Sensei Tsinelas
© 2025 Tanamor

ISBN13: 9781947845565

All rights reserved. No part of this book may be reproduced or transmitted in any form or by any means, electronic or mechanical, including photocopying, recording, or by any information storage and retrieval system, without permission in writing from the publisher.

Ooligan Press
Portland State University
Post Office Box 751, Portland, Oregon 97207
503.725.9748
ooligan@ooliganpress.pdx.edu
www.ooliganpress.com

Library of Congress Cataloging-in-Publication Data

Names: Tanamor, Jason, 1975- author.
Title: The Legend of Sensei Tsinelas / by Jason Tanamor.
Description: Portland : Ooligan Press, 2025. | Audience term: Teenagers |Audience: Ages 12-18. | Audience: Grades 10-12. | Summary: Seventeen-year-old Filipino American Victor Dela Cruz feels like an outsider at school, but when he sees his food truck boss use a tsinelas to stop a thief, his superhero obsession sparks a quest to uncover his boss's secret identity—while also learning to embrace his own cultural heritage.
Identifiers: LCCN 2024022921 | ISBN 9781947845565 (trade paperback) | ISBN 9781947845572 (ebook)
Subjects: CYAC: Self-acceptance—Fiction. | Puerto Ricans--Fiction. | Bullies and bullying--Fiction. | Superheroes--Fiction. | LCGFT: Novels.
Classification: LCC PZ7.1.T374 Le 2025 | DDC [Fic]--dc23
LC record available at https://lccn.loc.gov/2024022921

Cover design by Alexandra Devon
Interior design by Samantha Gallasch

References to website URLs were accurate at the time of writing. Neither the author nor Ooligan Press is responsible for URLs that have changed or expired since the manuscript was prepared.
Printed in the United States of America

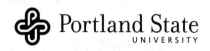

For the hero within all of us. Where the true power lies.

OOMCHA, OOMCHA, OOMCHA

Cleaning up Waterfront Park wasn't first on my list of fun ways to spend the last day of summer break. But what could I do? My boss, whom I'd only known as "Sir" since I began working for him three months ago, thought giving back to the community was necessary for business. One of the things he'd always say in his oftentimes choppy English was, "We serve the people. It why we exist." Whatever the case, this was what I was doing.

The mass of greenery along the waterfront was filled with walkways and a view of Portland's eastside. The park—blocks and blocks of perfectly manicured greenspace—ran along the Willamette River and was a shared spot for much of downtown.

It was where joggers convened to run in groups, picnickers gathered to spend time with their loved ones, and locals and tourists congregated to lose themselves in the calmness of the river. A few blocks up were shops and restaurants, so inevitably, the park was a mess. Like, trash everywhere.

The cleanup, facilitated by SOLVE Oregon, brought community members together to help keep Portland safe and beautiful. This was great and all, but the day was dragging on.

Sir was volunteering as well—which made the day more bearable—along with several dozen, maybe a hundred or so, locals doing their duty to the city. Some were other business owners in the area, and I recognized a few people from the food cart block I worked at. It was still early, so none of the eateries were even open yet. So that made sense.

Every so often, I'd see Sir in my peripheral, and I swore he was shooting or slinging trash into the cans like it was nothing. In my mind, there was something magical about how the debris and refuse were just floating into the bins. But every time I looked at him directly, he was tossing a crumpled bag into the waste basket just like any other volunteer. It only added to his mystique.

I wouldn't have suspected anything special about Sir—a.k.a. mild-mannered chef and owner of the best food cart in Portland: Filipino Feast—if it hadn't been for the heroic incident I'd witnessed during a closing shift.

Although it happened weeks ago, I remember like it was yesterday.

All was good until a commotion startled me to investigate. I was set to deliver some orders to nearby patrons within a block radius. By then the day was turning dark, and it was at that perfect in-between time where the sun was set but the darkness hadn't reared its head quite yet. Faces were blurred and shadows had become more prevalent. It was as if Portland proper suddenly became Gotham.

"Help!" a woman screamed. "Help, help!"

My gaze darted around the area until I spotted it—a robbery!

The woman was grasping onto her purse, pulling it back into herself with great force. On the other end was a disheveled man, tall and skinny, dressed in all black and wearing a beat-up baseball cap.

The purse's strap was stretching to its limit, only to recoil as the struggle between the robber and the victim continued like an awkward dance routine.

"Let go!" the robber screamed.

The few customers at Sir's window stopped in an instant and turned to observe the happenings. Any of them could have acted, myself included, but for whatever reason we watched in shock, our feet frozen to the ground.

Portland, like any other big city, had its share of crime, and this wasn't the first that I'd ever witnessed firsthand. Plus, with daily news reports containing multiple tragic stories, they didn't seem real to me anymore. *Just another television program*, I thought sadly, desensitized to my core.

"Help!" the woman screamed again. Small but feisty, she clutched her purse with all her strength. Her knuckles were turning pale from the constant effort to hold on.

I thought about acting. After all, I was wearing a Superman shirt for Christ's sake! I could do something about it. Be the hero! Place my fists on my hips, push out my chest, and save the day!

But . . . who was I kidding?

This shirt didn't give me any powers. If it did, every kid out there would be bending steel with his bare hands or stopping runaway trains before they fell off the tracks.

"Helllllllp!"

The mugger pulled out a knife and the woman's panic elevated.

"Take it, take it!" she screamed, pushing her purse toward him.

When it didn't look like there were any other options, a voice escaped the food cart's window.

It was Sir.

"*Ay nako!*"

I'd heard that phrase many times when Dad was annoyed or inconvenienced.

I screamed into the food cart's window, "What should we do?" The few collective heads looked in all directions searching for someone to come to the rescue. My request fell on deaf ears. "Sir!" I said. Sir's eyes found mine. "What should we do?"

Sir swallowed hard, and with a shaky smile, he motioned with his hand for his customers and me to move. The small gathering cleared at once, giving him a direct view of the perpetrator.

"*Susmaryosep*," he muttered. It was a Filipino phrase, slang for "Jesus, Mary, Joseph."

Sir kicked off one of his *tsinelas*—a ratty foam slipper—cut an uncertain glance at it, and then whipped it out like a boomerang. The slipper spun out of the small, rectangular-shaped cart's window and into the distance, curlicuing in the air—the sound of soft whistling combined with a smell of foam and feet—and pelted the robber in the head. The crook's ballcap fell to the ground. A few milliseconds later the crook followed, a surprised grunt of pain escaping him. Sir had knocked him unconscious. I couldn't believe it!

My eyes bulged. What the—?

A gasp was let out in the distance.

On the opposite side of me, someone said, "Whoa!"

We must have been thinking the same thing. No way!

The woman hugged her purse tightly, paused momentarily to look astonishingly above her head, and then ran the other way glancing behind her shoulder every few steps.

The slipper was still spinning in the air—whizzing a victory song (the upbeat *oomcha, oomcha, oomcha* tempo of a club song)—until it returned to the food cart, through the window, and into Sir's hand. Defying physics, the slipper had never hit the ground.

The event happened quickly, and before I could determine what'd happened, Sir was placing the slipper, ever so delicately, back onto his foot. He exhaled deeply in relief and returned to his casual self, as if nothing ever happened.

A woman cheered at Sir's long-range shot into the metal can. The clanking of the balled-up fast-food bag brought me back to the present, the image of the boomerang slipper fading from my memory. I was back in Waterfront Park. Sir nodded, his lips forming a gentle yet appreciative smile.

Another person attempted a similar shot from closer but missed wide.

If only I was as skilled and talented. I would be loved and revered. All the eyes would be on me. But it wasn't like I was one of those characters in every martial arts film ever made. Some secret prodigy discovered after he'd moved into town because his single parent had taken a job as an executive assistant or something. Forced to find new friends in a world where he didn't belong. Discovered while twisting soda cans into origami pretzels. A gifted kid of sorts.

Or appearing in Jonathan and Martha Kent's lives as a young baby with superpowers whom they find and name Clark.

I was nothing like that.

I was a nerd.

I was . . . me.

I shook my head, squinting as I looked toward the sun as it rose over Mt. Hood. The scene was fairytale-like, bringing together a cityscape, river, and mountain all at once, like a colorful painting across Portland's skyline. The sight made me smile despite my day doing chores.

Sir edged up next to me with a slight look of concern. His body cast a shadow over me like a superhero watching over the city.

"Victor," he said in a soft tone. "You okay?"

How long have I been sitting here?

"Just tired," I answered. "I don't know how you can work all day and night and then come out here and work again."

"It only been two hours," he said.

"It has?"

Sir chuckled.

"When people work together, it makes it fun," he said as he did some weird shimmy with his shoulders, side to side, until his own quirkiness overcame him and he stopped in what I thought was embarrassment. "Make it easy," he said, gesturing to the mass of people around us.

When he finished, he sat next to me, plopping his potato-shaped body onto the grass, his head slowly craning toward my direction.

"I understand that," I said. "I meant that you're much older than I am, and I'm exhausted."

"Much older? Or much more wise?"

"Sorry," I said. "Much more wise. I guess my wisdom level isn't as high as yours."

"Like energy level," said Sir. "Good one. Well, just try and have fun." He then rose to his feet and joined a group nearby. It was like he never broke a sweat.

Sir engaged the volunteers with his animated stories and charm, and I couldn't help but feel inadequate. How did he do it? He was so loved and revered. Me? I was a nerdy high school kid whose life revolved around superhero things. I didn't have any real friends, as keeping my grades up was tiring enough. Adding a part-time job and volunteer work? Well, that was just insane. How in the world would I ever keep up with all the superhero universes? In fact, my only friend was my kid sister whose spare time entailed learning all about our culture, and she took everything in stride, almost like she wanted to do more. I guess her wisdom level was much higher than mine too.

I looked down at the Captain America symbol on my T-shirt. It mocked me. He was the field commander. The leader of the Avengers. The one who everyone looked up to. It was almost as if Sir should have been wearing this shirt.

I raised my chin as I rested—the aches and pain beginning to swelter across my body—and I watched my boss steal the show. With his affable demeanor and never-ending supply of energy—er, wisdom—coupled with the incident that I'd witnessed, there was no doubt about it:

Sir is a modern-day superhero!

TO BE A SUPERHERO

I always preferred the train's stop that was smack dab in the center of downtown Portland. It was amid everything—commerce, tourism, and food—and adjacent to Pioneer Square, the large plaza in the middle of the city center known as Portland's Living Room.

My house was just off West Burnside Street, past the section where the highway spanned below the overpass. It was a modest-sized two-story house, the only house I'd ever known, cramped into a tiny cul-de-sac whose street seemed to twist into another cul-de-sac, which wound its way up into the hills of northwest Portland. It was my safe place or, in other words, my fortress of solitude. Just like Superman.

The four houses in our court were all snug together, making the small neighborhood an even tighter community. You couldn't tell my house from the next one. It was very boring, the opposite of Pioneer Square.

This morning, I walked with my sister, Ginessa, down the sloped street and into downtown, through the city center—passing an array of retail shops, food carts, and trendy restaurants—to hop on the Orange Line for school. It was the first week of the school year at Cleveland High, but more importantly, it was Ginessa's freshman year.

I couldn't afford a car and Ginessa wasn't old enough to drive yet, so public transportation was our only way. It wasn't horrible, mainly because I was a senior, seventeen going on adulthood, and once I graduated, I'd rarely take the train again. At least to school. My part-time job consisted of running errands across downtown, delivering food to various residents and businesses within the city center, and working the counter.

For the most part, I liked taking orders but not necessarily making small talk with customers. That was Sir's bread and butter.

Ginessa, an extroverted teenager who had an unlimited outlook on life, *loved* going to school. But it wasn't just school. She looked forward to life in general, even simple things like chatting with the neighbors or catching up with the mail carrier, and much to my dismay, it was this outlook that got her to the same point each school day: talking endlessly about issues that, if ever a poll of caring about things had existed, ranked low in my life.

Her topic this morning was the annual Filipino-American picnic that was approaching. The association served Portland and its suburbs, bringing together residents of Filipino descent to share in the one thing that Filipinos loved the most: food.

Well, Filipinos loved other things—karaoke, Mahjong, dancing, family—but the one thing that brought us together was food. You could be sitting alone, with no Filipinos within a hundred-mile radius, but once that rice cooker lever popped, you'd be surrounded by faux aunties and uncles as if they'd been singing karaoke in the next room.

The picnic was one of the biggest events of the season. This year it would be held at a public park in the northeast part of Portland, but it would change locations next year to accommodate those who live in different quadrants of the city. One year, it was a short walking distance from our house, but since then, it had hopped around the city. Wherever it was, Ginessa always planned on attending even if the train commute took over an hour.

With my chin down, gaze focused on the sidewalk in front of me, we headed to the train's stop.

Slung around my shoulders was my backpack stuffed with comic books.

The bag's light weight caused me to readjust the backpack, the thin superhero books sliding around making it feel super light. It was almost as if wearing an Incredible Hulk T-shirt gave me strength.

My body was lanky and with little definition. What I had for arms and legs looked like dry spaghetti; there were no muscles whatsoever. My longish, dark brown hair, unkempt most of the time, covered my brown-skinned face to the point where I had to jerk my neck for my bangs to move off my slanted eyes.

I didn't care though. It sheltered me from the world, protecting me. Like Hal Jordan hiding his Green Lantern identity, I tried to stay unnoticed.

I'd always wanted to be a superhero. That was my dream—having superpowers like Superman or some arsenal of special skills like Batman. Being something extraordinary, unique. Being loved and revered.

"I'm hoping somebody brings *hopia*," said Ginessa.

I noticed a wide smile stretched across her face and her eyes were flashing; I wasn't sure why. My mind was somewhere else.

"I said, 'I'm hoping somebody brings hopia,'" Ginessa repeated.

"Oh," I remarked. "That sounds good."

Ginessa closed her eyes.

"I can taste the mung beans now as the crust flakes off with each bite," she said. The tip of her tongue protruded from her lips. She was so into the imaginary pastry that she almost tripped over herself.

"Hopia *is* good," I confirmed. *Are we still talking about the picnic? When is it again?* "Man, I haven't had that in a while," I remembered, pushing out a smile. "But I *do* know a good place that sells them." My vision turned toward Ginessa, and my eyes flashed in jubilation.

"That's right!" she said.

"Maybe we can go after school."

"Maybe."

Ginessa was just as skinny as I was, her knees and elbows bony like golf balls attached to toothpicks, and she walked with a slight awkwardness. Clumsily was more like it. Her dark, straight hair was pinned back in a ponytail, thick and tight—a look that took her only a couple of seconds to perfect. Her bangs rested above her eyebrows, trimmed perfectly straight. She almost looked like an action movie villain, or some powerful superhero with the whole world at her disposal: sweet and innocent but probably could kick your butt. And her outfit, she always wore a *baro't saya*, a Filipino style comprised of some sort of blouse and skirt.

Although Mom tried hard to instill culture into us, I'd never wear something so ethnic, not in a million years. But Ginessa? She was just comfortable being herself. The first day of school resulted in mostly stares (none of which even bothered her), and after day three, kids just stopped caring.

Again, I turned toward Ginessa.

"You can always make hopia too, ya know?"

Suddenly, Ginessa pouted.

What did I say?

Her shoulders dropped as if I'd let the air out of her. I pictured her body collapsing into itself, deflating before my very eyes like a balloon with a slight puncture.

Sinking into herself, she frowned.

"Mom was going to show me how to make it one day, but . . ." Her voice trailed off. "It just never happened."

"I-I'm sorry," I said, kicking myself internally for reminding her of our mother.

I ground my teeth, my lips tightening together. I couldn't stand to look at Ginessa, even though I was older and was supposed to be the mature one of the family—the man of the house—so I kept my gaze on the ground in front of me.

"It's okay," said Ginessa. "I know you're just trying to help." Her shoulders fell in defeat. "I really miss her, though."

"I do too," I whispered.

LEADER OF THE FILIPINOS

Even though summer break had just ended, I couldn't wait for it to come back around. I didn't have any real plans; rather, I just wanted to get away from classrooms and homework. And from the other kids. Let's be real: nobody liked nerdy boys like Peter Parker, who was once a science teacher, or someone into technical specs like Hal Jordan, a former fighter pilot. They loved their alter egos: Spiderman and Green Lantern. I was the former because if you needed someone to ace a test for you with hardly any studying, I was your guy.

Although Ginessa looked forward to school, she also was anxious for summer break, but she had different motives. She was excited to dedicate her time learning about our heritage via the Portland chapter of the Filipino-American Association. Her two friends, Elena and Denise, loved our food and culture. This inspired Ginessa to learn even more so she could teach them things.

Mom always made it a point to speak Tagalog to Ginessa, ensuring she was exposed to our culture. She didn't force the language onto her like she'd forced it on me when I was younger, maybe hoping that Ginessa would be more receptive to learning than I was. It seemed to have taken though, as oftentimes I would hear Ginessa speaking Taglish with Lola. For being educated on an informal level, Ginessa was semi-fluent.

Lola, our maternal grandmother, was now raising us and doing the best she could with the Mahjong tiles she was dealt. She had a newfound responsibility raising her grandchildren. So, to relieve the pressure that Lola faced, Ginessa called upon the other Filipinos in the area to help fill the void, like a Filipino bat-signal in the air! They rose to the occasion, and in the truest Filipino love language ever, showered our family with gifts, money, and a variety of food dishes.

Now, Ginessa had a good combination of resources.

Ginessa had marked the date on her calendar when the association first announced the picnic. Since the school year had begun, the event became a talking point on our trek to school each morning.

"What if you made one of your famous adobo dishes?" I suggested with the perfect amount of indifference. Frankly, I wasn't invested in the conversation, but it was a way to kill time, and appease her simultaneously. Be the good brother.

"Nah," dismissed Ginessa. "There'll probably be a hundred different versions of adobo there. Pork, chicken, you name it." She curled her bottom lip under her front teeth and looked toward the sky. It looked like she was asking for approval or perhaps a suggestion, but I wasn't sure.

I joined her, staring up into the sky. The day was cloudy, the forecast calling for clearing later and into the week. Each cloud looked the same as the others, and nothing or no one called out to me. I wasn't certain what Ginessa was doing so I continued to stare aimlessly.

"I'm actually thinking about making a flan," she said, her attention drifting toward my direction, "or some sort of side, dessert-y dish." She pondered this for a second, her eyes shrinking and her brows wrinkling as her mind, once again, became lost in uncertainty. Then she came to a conclusion. "Nah, a flan. But I'll have to doublecheck the sheet." Tapping her chin with her finger, she said, "And do I even have the ingredients?"

I shrugged even though the question was rhetorical.

The picnic was taking place a few Saturdays from now. Ginessa sat on the organization's board and, this year, oversaw the spreadsheet that said who was bringing what dish. She was the youngest member to hold an officer's position and her dream was to be president of the association one day. She'd mentioned numerous times—jokingly perhaps—that she wanted to be leader of the Filipinos. It always made her giggle.

Once Ginessa was finished talking, I turned my lips down, and with a shaky smile, I said, "I'm thinking about skipping this year's picnic."

Ginessa's eyes widened and she stopped short.

"What? You can't skip it!" she said.

"I'm a teenager. I'm busy," I replied, feeling just a bit snarky. "Plus, I have a job."

My beating heart thumped hard against my chest. It was a lie because I knew that if I asked for the day off, I could have it, but I didn't want her to know.

"But it only comes once a year," Ginessa protested. "You can't miss it!" She whipped her head around to glare at me, her eyes burning into my soul like high-temperature laser beams ready to melt me into nothing. "Request that day off! It's a chance to see all our framily."

"Framily?"

"Friends and family," she said. "Geez, Victor. Get with it!"

I pressed my lips tightly into a thin line. I really didn't want to go. Even though it'd been almost a year, I couldn't deal with all the people consoling us, pitying us with their look-at-those-kids expressions. It would be too much for me.

Also, I didn't want to be around that many Filipinos at once. It was bad enough being a brown kid in a mostly white city. Being around a bunch of Filipinos felt like being a fish in an aquarium where everyone was just staring at you. Like, look at *these people*. It would feel like my family tree project came to life, and there was no way I wanted to relive that again.

"All of Mom and Dad's friends, you mean," I said, craning my head to look at Ginessa, my heart sinking as my eyes locked into hers. "I just don't want to go through that again."

"That's why it's important that we go," said Ginessa, her voice soft and shaky, her innocence creeping past her anger. "Aside from Lola, these people are our family."

A slight pang of guilt ran through me. I had to stay firm.

"But they *aren't* our family."

"They're Filipinos," cried Ginessa. "All Filipinos are"—she made air quotes with her fingers—"family."

I exhaled in frustration. Ginessa's eyes began to water.

"Lola's going," I offered.

"But it won't be the same."

Just then, a car flew past us. It was sleek, silver, and luxurious, a fancy sports car of some sort, traveling above the posted speed limit like it owned the road—and maybe it did.

A faint voice escaped the passenger seat.

"Nerd!" it screamed. There was some audible laughter. I eyed the car as an arm extended out the driver's side window and gave us the finger. I knew exactly who owned it from the sticker plastered on the right side of the car's bumper. The sticker had the school's logo and a football jersey boasting a certain number on it. A certain number belonging to a certain quarterback who continually picked on me and those like me: Clint Robertson. Riding shotgun, undoubtedly, was his sidekick, Bart.

Inside, I silently fumed. Before my anger consumed me, I imagined my arm stretching super long like Mr. Fantastic and reaching out until it grabbed the car's rear bumper. My entire body was elastic, and part of my superhero repertoire was the ability to contort my body into different shapes, like a rubber band in this case. Stretching the limit, a loud ripping sound echoing in the air, my body was no longer recognizable.

When my grasp was tight enough, I yanked the car back in its wheels.

SCREECH!

The sudden brake caused Clint and Bart to fly through the windshield and land in a conveniently placed dumpster onto the street. Spectators pointed in slack-jawed amazement! Not at the bullies climbing out of the garbage, but at my rubber arm retracting back to normal, flailing like a streamer until it was back to its normal length. Whispers and murmurs filled the air.

My body instantly brightened from the trance. If only. I merely shook my head and said nothing.

Ginessa, however, screamed at the car with all her lungs and forcefulness.

"Do that to my face!" she yelled. It was now far enough away for nothing to come of it.

But still, my mouth dropped open, an instinct I'd grown accustomed to. My eyes dashed from the receding car to my sister. I cupped my hand around Ginessa's mouth, covering it.

"Are you crazy?" I said with a trembling voice. "You're going to get my butt kicked."

"From here?" She looked up the street, where the car's tiny taillights were disappearing, and the din of the engine dissipated as she spoke.

What if they have superhuman hearing?

"What is wrong with you?" asked Ginessa.

"Um . . . nothing," I said as she snaked out of my grasp.

"Then why are you acting this way?"

"What way?"

She stared at me with narrowed eyes.

"I don't know," she said. "Like this!" Then she placed her palm over her lips and dramatically raised her eyebrows at me. When I said nothing, she released her grip. "He literally just gave you the finger, and you did nothing."

"I was . . ." My gaze drifted.

"Never mind."

Shaking her head, Ginessa stomped forward, leaving me to lag. I could tell she was disappointed in me because the rest of the walk was quiet. Also, Ginessa increased her pace to gain distance on me. We didn't say a word when the train arrived.

YOU WOULDN'T LIKE ME

Although this was the first week, everything seemed to gray and darken as if I had suddenly walked down a pitch-black alley. Like I was an unsuspecting victim in a comic book. Maybe I was.

My stomach dropped as we approached the building, sinking deeper and deeper into a pit. The entrance was busy with incoming kids, each melding into a narrow line as they disappeared into the school. Laughter hit the air, followed by chitchat. For me, seeing Clint and Bart drive by, it was a potential continuation of last year, and the year before.

Ginessa was gaining distance from me, never once looking to see how far I'd fallen behind. By the way she was stomping off, I could tell she was still irritated by my cowardice. When she was in junior high, it was much easier to hide my personal life from her. But with us now attending the same school, she would finally see me for who I really was.

She was a few cars' length ahead of me (not small, compact cars, but long, old school Cadillacs or stretch limos), walking quicker and quicker as she began to morph into the line of kids entering the school.

Finally, calling out to her, I said, "Wait up!" I increased my stride until I caught up with her.

Kids filled the rest of the school grounds, all meandering to the front door to begin their respective days. Just under two thousand students attended. As soon as I reached the entryway, a mass of kids surrounded me, shoulder to shoulder, and it made my stomach feel rock hard.

Ginessa exhaled.

"Why would I? You acted all weird back there, and when I asked you what was wrong, you flaked." She leaned in closer to me. "So . . ."

I started to answer but then I stopped when one of Ginessa's eyebrows began to raise. I swallowed what little saliva I had in my mouth. Her one eyebrow always frightened me. It had a mind of its own, distinct from any body part that Ginessa had. This was a trait she'd inherited from Mom. No matter how high on her forehead it raised, it always led to the same thing—that I was about to lie.

Her eyebrow, inching up until it rested halfway up her forehead, wasn't too damning.

"So . . ." she repeated, more clipped this time.

A classmate bumped into me, spinning me off balance. Any harder and I would have spun into the floor like a drill.

"Sorry," the boy said in the distance, and then faint laughter ensued. I followed the voice, a football player I guessed from my glance—he was shaped like the rest of them—disappeared down the hall.

A few moments later, another fit of laughter. This time, it was faint. I could tell that he'd found his next victim.

I imagined a bad guy theme in a high-budget, summer blockbuster but quickly dismissed the picture as I caught sight of Ginessa glaring down the hall. She had no idea the football players made fun of me for being a nerdy, smart kid.

"Did that boy just ram you on purpose?"

"I don't think so," I said, pointing in the direction of where the classmate had disappeared.

"He hit you pretty hard," she said. "That couldn't have been an accident."

"It's no big deal," I quickly dismissed, a defense mechanism I'd used for the umpteenth time of my high school life when it pertained to that crowd. Normally, I was a low-key, fairly confident student, but my insecurity got the best of me with the popular kids. I just wanted to fit in. I wanted them to like me . . . but I would settle for them just ignoring me.

My head dropped, my eyes closing to hide the shame. I spun around to continue forward when, suddenly, my arm bumped into Clint—yes, *that* Clint! He was a football player, the starting quarterback, Mr. Popularity, the villain who had bullied kids like me for many years.

The force from my arm knocked the cappuccino Clint was clutching.

My brain suddenly shut down, and instantly, I imagined I was in la-la land. I raised both palms up, focused on the catapulted liquid, and screamed, "Freeze!"

The drink froze in mid-air, locked in the shape of a waterfall creeping over its edge.

Bystanders stared at the scene like I was Tobey Maguire as Peter Parker, waiting for me to catch the liquid into a cup like he did with Mary Jane's tray of food.

Clint's eyes bulged as he leaned in closer and touched it, careful not to disrupt whatever phenomenon was currently happening.

"What the—" he said to himself.

All eyes fell upon me, the great superhero who somehow was able to do extraordinary things. Someone behind me screamed something to the effect that I was a wizard or demon of some sort.

Another classmate nearby uttered, "It's not moving."

A nearby girl said, "I'm scared."

But that wasn't what happened. Not even close. In reality, the coffee spilled onto another jock standing next to him.

The hot drink spilled in slow motion, their expressions displaying a clear frame-by-frame indifference transforming into anger. The fear within pushed up from my gut, and I nearly vomited.

"What the hell?" screamed Bart. He inspected the brown coffee stain that was expanding on his shirt. "I just got this shirt!" Clenching his jaw, he stood red-faced. He smudged the stain with his fingertips, attempting to lessen the impact with quick, short strokes. A vein crisscrossed his forehead, raising almost an inch high off his head to express his rage.

Bart was the same height as me, but he was cut like a sculpture that stood in front of a museum. Not a children's museum or a fancy art museum where the sculptures are just tall, lopsided flowers made from tin, but a museum in the heart of New York City or Italy, or any other art mecca.

While Bart tended to the stain, Clint, on the other hand, got in my face.

"I paid *good* money for that cappuccino," he said, a faint scent of milk hitting me. A collective "ooh" from the surrounding kids traveled around me like a fan wave at a baseball stadium. Eying my shirt, he smirked. "Did you hear that, Hulk?"

I should have responded with a smart-aleck comment, something the Hulk's secret identity, Bruce Banner, would say, like, "Don't make me angry. You wouldn't like me when I'm angry." But I didn't. The truth was, Clint was a human tree. Not a Charlie Brown Christmas tree, but the kind that the city of Portland lights up every day after Thanksgiving for the entire city to admire: a seventy-five-foot Douglas fir.

Of course, Clint wasn't *that* tall, but he did stand six-feet-something in height and was built like a bulldozer. He was the quintessential all-American teen, with blond hair, dreamy blue eyes, and dimples that stretched his cheeks. His teeth were whiter than my Lola's rice, and his smile made the entire student body's knees buckle. It subliminally read, "You can trust me." All the girls fawned over him, and all the guys wanted to be him. All these traits worked in his favor at his parents' car dealership where he made appearances after school, I imagined.

"Are you going to do something about it, Hulk?" He lengthened his torso, extending his chest out to me, attempting to provoke me into a fight. "Huh?"

My heart started to race. Scanning the classmates' looks, I swallowed hard. They stared at me like wild animals in the night, sending chills up and down my spine, and I tried to escape the torture by slinking backward.

In my mind, I was the Flash, suddenly hightailing out of there at a zillion miles per hour. But instead of standing up for myself, I did what I did best: I relented. Instantly, the knack to avoid violence spilled out like a confession to the FBI, and I blabbered senselessly with hopes that everything would just go away.

"I'll buy you another one," I said.

Bart's nostrils flared.

"You're going to pay for a new shirt too," he said, scanning the stain. By now, it had settled into a nice splotch in the center of his chest. The stain hadn't blended nearly as nice as Bart would have liked, and it was shaped like a small country that, in this case, exported coffee.

Ginessa, though, did not cower. She did nothing of the sort. Instead, she rolled up her proverbial sleeves and instantly sprang into action, her eyes narrowing as she got a better look at Clint.

"Why would he have to buy you another coffee?" she said. "It was an accident."

I nudged her with my elbow, shushing her under my breath.

Clint's nose wrinkled, his gaze locking onto hers.

"It—it's fine," I lied, and then I eyed Ginessa and slowly nodded.

"That's not right!" Ginessa snarled, not getting the hint whatsoever. *Kid sisters*, I thought. *I swear.* She turned to Bart. "Victor shouldn't have to buy you a new shirt."

Clenching my teeth, I silently pleaded for her to shut up.
Ginessa locked her gaze on Clint.
"And he shouldn't have to replace your drink." She turned to address me. Everyone did, including Clint and Bart. I was standing statue still (and let me remind you, not a statue like Bart; it was more like a statue made from papier-mâché at a children's museum), my eyes wider than a full moon. "Just say you're sorry," she said. "That should be good enough."

Clint viciously eyed me. He smirked, his stare dancing between me and Ginessa.

"You know what?" he said. "To prevent embarrassing you in front of your sister, who clearly needs to defend you, we'll continue this later."

Then they walked away.

I turned to see Ginessa staring at me. I could tell her brain was working, putting two and two together.

"Was that the guy in the car from earlier?" she asked.

"I don't want to talk about it."

"It was, wasn't it?"

I stared down the hall and watched the group of football players. The halls had cleared a bit with each classmate finding their classroom, leaving a clear visual of Clint and Bart. A few other jocks ambled around, and one kid stood in front of his locker, digging out a notebook in a frenzy.

Clint's demeanor lightened and he playfully bantered with Bart and his other teammates.

"C'mon," I urged. "Let's go."

I started walking toward her classroom. Ginessa followed me, and when we got there, she rounded in front of me, stopped, and looked me square in the face.

"I didn't know you got bullied," she said, pausing to find the next words. "Why didn't you say something? Mom and Dad didn't raise us this way."

This sort of took me by surprise because it wasn't something that I'd really considered. She was right. Our parents had always taught us to stand up for ourselves. But when your bullies were ten times the size of you, did you really have a choice?

"Maybe we can talk about this later," said Ginessa.

Perhaps.

She smiled and disappeared into the classroom. After a few steps, she turned to address me.

"I'll see you after school?"

Nodding, I said, "Of course."

A few seconds later, I hurriedly found my own class down a couple of halls and then skulked to the desk in the front of the room. Looking at the clock on the wall, I sighed. It was only first period, and I already wished the day was over.

HAVE YOU TRIED BALUT?

We headed to the train stop after school.

Afternoon commuters packed tight into the train, causing us to separate into single seats next to random commuters heading to God knows where. The computerized voice announced our stop, and once we exited the train, I said, "Let's grab some Filipino food."

By now, the day had warmed to a nice sixty-five or so degrees, and when the sun hit, the balminess was a soft embrace against my face. A pool of sweat had formed under my hairline on the stuffed train. I whipped my neck to brush my hair away from my eyes.

"After today, I'm feeling *halo-halo*," I said.

Ginessa's eyes lit up, her happiness finding its way into my soul, and I smiled. She had our mother's face and it made me think about her.

She rubbed her palms together in excitement. From my knowledge, she hadn't had halo-halo since the last picnic. It was a staple there.

"I take that as a 'yes'?"

Her eyes widening, she nodded.

"Come on," I said. "I'll take you to my work."

"Awesome!" she said. "It would be cool to see Sir again."

I chuckled.

"Yeah, he's pretty cool."

"Do you even know his real name?" she asked. "You always refer to him as Sir."

I shrugged.

"I don't." And then I laughed. "Plus," I started, looking around us to ensure no one was listening, "I think he's a superhero."

"Maybe that's why you don't know his real name," quipped Ginessa.

I dismissed her and then my voice fell into a soft whisper, and I began telling her this incredible backstory that I imagined about how Sir secretly lives inside some underground base where he has rows of outfits and an arsenal of weapons that span the walls. On a screen above a massive control panel was a bird's eye view of downtown Portland. He could zoom in on any area with precision, picking up faces to identify them in a heartbeat.

At night—

Ginessa laughed out loud, hysterically, and the sound of it broke my concentration.

"A superhero? I mean, that would be so awesome if that were true! But, c'mon!"

My excitement was short-lived. I shook off the accusation feeling a little embarrassed.

"Yeah, you're probably right."

"I'm sure he'd love to hear this theory," she said. "Have you ever talked to him about it?"

"Oh, God, no!" I replied. "We don't talk about stuff like that. Just random stuff about work. It's mostly superficial." Excitement hit me. "Although one time . . ." I told her about Sir throwing one of his tsinelas which foiled the robbery.

I wasn't certain if she believed me, but soon after, we arrived at my work.

The cart's exterior was decorated by scanned pictures of the Philippines—beaches, mountains, and outdoor markets—and the country's flag draped from the top of the wooden kitchen.

Sir greeted us in his typical jovial demeanor. It was one I'd grown accustomed to. And come to think of it, it was very . . . secret identity-ish.

There wasn't another employee aside from me, and the only reason Sir offered me a job was because I was Filipino. So he said, at least. I'd first discovered the food cart when I was missing Mom's cooking. It was something just to remind me of home. After talking to Sir, he was amazed that I knew so little about our culture. Then, after a few minutes of what felt like training, he asked if I wanted to work. I honestly didn't even think he needed me, but I jumped at the opportunity to make some money and distract myself from school.

"Ah, *kumusta!*" he said. Then he slid over a row of Mahjong tiles he'd been messing with to the edge of the counter.

I'd never actually seen Sir play Mahjong. I'd seen the tiles several times but in different formations, somewhat like Legos. One time, he spelled out the word "FOOD" on the counter's ledge.

Sir was a middle-aged Filipino man, maybe in his late forties or early fifties, who owned and operated the cart specializing in authentic Filipino dishes. He was potato-shaped, with the thickest girth appearing in his belly, which protruded well past his beltline. Overall, he was round and jolly looking, like a Filipino Santa Claus. If I had to sum him up in one word, he was unassuming.

The food cart sat in a premiere location downtown, in the middle of where tourists frequented most, co-mingling with other carts within the largest food cart block in the city.

Although the cart was small and compact, there were tiny nooks that we used to jam supplies into to manage a full day's worth of meals. The cabinets and drawers looked like an emergency bunker for an earthquake that hadn't happened yet. Items were stored precisely in place to maximize the area.

The sink was in between the window and kitchen area so that both Sir and I could wash our hands as needed. He designed this with the most efficiency in mind.

The kitchenette was wrapped around the back half of the truck, where Sir could bounce from the stovetop to the refrigerator and from the fryer to the prep counter. Even though the space was tight, he navigated the area like a ballet dancer, spinning one way and then pirouetting the other. Never once did he ruin any meals.

When the cart was closed for the day, Sir prepped the food (sometimes into the wee hours of the morning) in his tiny underground bunker—er, apartment in the Pearl District—just a few blocks away and carried it to the cart each morning to serve.

Smiling, Ginessa said, "Hello, Sir."

Sir put his hands together in prayer and then bowed. His head nearly touched the wooden counter and his horseshoe-patterned baldness grew larger when it neared me. To be honest, he looked uncomfortable. Any farther and Sir would be stuck in this position. But he managed to stand erect and greet us with a smile like every other day.

"Pleasure to see you again," he said to Ginessa.

Ginessa, for the pure sake of following suit, returned a bow of her own.

Sir returned his attention to me.

"You come on day off?" he questioned, displaying a confused look. "Or you working so I can leave early?" Then he chuckled.

"Just got out of school."

"I know, I know," he said. Then he winked at Ginessa.

"We're on our way home, but we decided to get something to eat first."

"You come to right place," Sir said as his glossy eyes panned from me to Ginessa. "What would you like, young lady?"

He stuck his head out the food cart's window and pointed to the menu that sprawled across the front of the cart. There was halo-halo, hopia, balut, barbecue shish kebabs, siopao (a bread-type roll made of wheat flour), lumpia and egg rolls, various types of adobo, a sticky rice dessert called suman, and pancit noodle-type dishes which comprised of either thin or thick noodles and vegetables. A meat, poultry, or type of seafood often complemented the pancit. I personally liked mine with chicken. Dad preferred shrimp, as did Ginessa. Mom, though, she preferred hers with both.

Come to think of it, I wondered if she didn't want to choose sides. So, instead, she chose both options.

The thick noodles were king in our home so there wasn't ever a question on which noodles to buy. I couldn't imagine Mom eating both thick *and* thin noodles, so I felt as if she'd escaped this dilemma.

The menu was written in erasable ink, and each morning, even though the items never rotated, Sir wrote the dishes in his best calligraphy.

"I have freshly made lumpia, both chicken and pork adobo," he offered, looking back at his current inventory of hot dishes.

Ginessa licked her lips. The smell of simmering soy sauce wafted in front of us, and she inhaled the aroma with open nostrils.

"All of it," she said, displaying a smile that reached her eyes.

"Let him finish," I said.

"All of it!"

I laughed and then reached into my pocket. Pulling out some random dollars, I counted them carefully. Crap! There wasn't enough to pay, and I frowned.

"I only have enough for one dish, even with my discount," I said to Ginessa with a deflated tone.

She sighed.

"I really wanted adobo," she replied. Her chin lowered in disappointment.

I shrugged.

"Sorry," I whispered. "I don't have it. Plus, I thought we came for hopia and halo-halo."

Whispering was not enough, though. Sir had sensed the entire conversation. Could it be his superhuman hearing? Or his superpower of reading lips? Could he have read our minds?

"Whatever you want," he said. "On the cart." Then he looked around the area to ensure that no one was within earshot. It was the I'll-hook-you-up-because-you're-Filipino discount that all Filipinos extended to one another. Seriously, it was a thing. Ask a Filipino. They probably wouldn't admit it because, well, it was a secret.

"No," I said. "I can't let you do that."

"Do what?" he shrugged. "You employee. I'm the boss, so I make the rules." Sir, whose head was still sticking partially out the cart's opening, continued to look down the sidewalk on both sides. "Plus, you hungry. I have food. What's the problem?"

I didn't want to take advantage of my boss or offend him. If there is one thing Filipinos got offended over, it was not eating food when offered. Even *I* knew that.

Sly in my approach, I said, "What if you take it out of my next paycheck?"

"You get paid?" said Filipino Santa. I chuckled. "Fine, whatever you need. If not, that all right too."

I wasn't going to win this time, no matter how hard I tried.

"Okay," I capitulated. "But I'm paying you back, some way."

Ginessa raised her fists in victory.

"Yay!"

Sir did as well, joining in on the celebration.

"Whatever you want," Sir offered.

Licking her lips, Ginessa said, "In that case, I want to try something I've never had."

"Hmm," Sir said. Then his eyes flashed. "I know. Have you tried balut?"

Suddenly, my eyes bulged to the size of beach balls. I dropped a step or two back behind Ginessa so she couldn't see me shaking my head. Raising my palms, I covertly waved Sir off.

"No, no, no," I mouthed.

Sir's gaze drifted toward me, his eyebrows drawing.

"Never mind. Your brother says no," he said. Then he imitated me by shaking his head erratically, his lips quaking to themselves. He giggled.

Ginessa's head whipped toward me. I swore I heard a loud *WHOOSH!* She didn't understand the joke.

She wore a slight scowl, but before she could speak, I said, "You won't like it. Trust me."

"Will you at least tell me what it is?" she asked. "Let me make up my own mind. If it's a Filipino dish, I want to know about it."

I wasn't sure that she did.

"I don't know," I answered. Then, sighing, I caught Sir's eyes.

"C'mon, what's the big deal?" She gently slapped my arm to get my attention. "What is it?"

My bottom lip curled under my front teeth, stalling for the best approach.

"You really want to try it?" I asked. She nodded. "Alright. But don't say I didn't warn you."

Sir reached behind him, dug into the small refrigerator, and pulled out an egg. It was a regular old egg, one that you could find at any grocery store. Seemingly. He then handed it over to Ginessa.

Ginessa observed it, turning it around as if a magical door to Narnia would suddenly open. Her eyebrows were caterpillars twisting across her forehead, pondering the inside joke she clearly wasn't a part of. She placed the egg under her nose, as if an aroma would give her a hint.

Nothing.

She shook it and listened to it like something would clue her in. As if a tiny voice would whisper, "Hello. I've been expecting you."

Still nothing.

She hesitated to make the connection, looking at me and then at Sir. After a thorough inspection of the egg, she gave up.

"I don't get it," she said, her face now scrunching into itself. "Why wouldn't I like an egg?"

Smiling, I shrugged.

Ginessa held up the egg in front of her, careful not to drop it, and then turned to Sir. Sir retrieved the egg, cracked it open on the wooden counter that hung over the window's ledge, split the egg in half, and then showed the contents to Ginessa.

I smirked hardcore, so much so I had to turn my head so she wouldn't see my face.

Ginessa, though, stepped back in horror. Her lips parted dramatically, and a gasp escaped her mouth. And I swore I heard her whisper-scream, "What the?" She covered her lips with her palm.

"What—what is that?" she said, pointing to the egg's insides.

She stepped closer to the cart's window to get a better look. We both did.

"It's balut," said Sir.

Inside the egg was a duck fetus, gestated for two to three weeks. Its little beak and eyeball were squished into its legs. Its darkish body, premature and fragile, curled into itself, and a hint of yellowing yolk surrounded the inside perimeter of the shell.

Ginessa swallowed hard. Her face crumpled in disgust and the skin around her cheeks suddenly paled. I chuckled to myself.

"It's a duck fetus," Sir explained. "It's boiled, then you eat it." He smelled the embryo, then tasted it with the tip of his tongue.

Ginessa winced.

"D-d-duck?"

"Yes," he said. "It's Filipino delicacy." He jokingly offered it back to Ginessa, who stumbled backward as she willfully declined with waving hands. His shoulders popped up and he slurped out the gooey broth of the egg that surrounded the embryo. He peeled back the shell, scooping out the yolk and egg white and then threw the contents into his mouth.

Ginessa's tongue jutted from her mouth and she swallowed hard.

"I don't think I'd like to try that," said Ginessa, placing her hand on her chest, feeling the pace of her heartbeat finish the final meter of a sprint. "But thank you."

"I told you," I said, shaking my head. "Didn't believe me."

It was settled. When Ginessa said she wanted all of it, she wanted both chicken and pork adobo. And lumpia. And pancit. And some hopia. And, ooh, some halo-halo. But not balut. *Definitely* not balut. No way!

The orders went through, and Sir asked Ginessa what she wanted in her halo-halo. The drink was a cool, refreshing dessert made up of ice, evaporated milk, and various ingredients that differed from person to person.

"What is there?"

"Anything you want," said Sir. "I got it!"

Without hesitation, Ginessa said, "I want coconut strips, black beans, gummi worms, flan, and bits of *ube*."

I jerked my head back. Her lessons in Filipino culture were paying off.

"Attagirl," said Sir. "Good choice."

Sir then turned to me.

"You?" he asked.

"I'll do the same."

"Give me couple minutes." Sir disappeared into the cart and began preparing the orders.

Ginessa looked at me.

"This is so exciting," she said. She rubbed her hands together in anticipation.

"You're going to love it," I said. I looked to Sir, who was packaging up the meals, and I felt guilty for accepting the food.

He returned to the window with a plastic bag filled with stacked cardboard containers. He slid over the orders.

"Here you are," he said. "Be careful, the lumpia is hot. Maybe wait a few minutes before eating."

Distracted by the decorations, Ginessa said, "I love how bedazzled your cart is."

A smile spread across Sir's face.

"I like how you interested in the Philippines." Then his eyes drew to mine. "Why not teach this one?" He pointed at me with his lips and then chuckled.

Ginessa joined in on the teasing.

"Been trying," she replied. "Trust me." Her eyebrows creased. "Speaking of the Philippines, how come I've never seen you at the Filipino picnic?"

"I always busy here."

She glanced around the cart and its surrounding area.

"I get that. Well, maybe you'll find time to come to the picnic this year," she offered. "It's coming up."

"Maybe."

Leaning in close to Ginessa, I whispered, "Told you. He's too busy fighting crime."

Ginessa smiled and gathered the orders, squeezing her wrist through the bag's handle and collecting the two cups of halo-halo.

"On the cart," he snickered until his shoulders began to shake.

"I'm paying you back!" I responded but Sir continued to laugh.

Ginessa and I walked to the train stop, an evening's worth of Filipino food in hand.

"That was nice of him," Ginessa said.

"Yeah," I replied. "And don't worry about all that back there with the balut. That's what happened when I first started. It scared the crap outta me."

"Look at you," she said. "You knew something about the Philippines that I didn't."

I shook my head.

"That's the stuff we talk about," I answered.

"I hear ya," said Ginessa. "It's probably a lot more productive than superhero things."

Ginessa scooped a bite of her halo-halo and swallowed slowly.

Licking her lips, she said, "But I can see what you're talking about. He's nice, *very modest*. He talks about food during work at a food cart. So, he could be a superhero. A superhero whose powers are cooking super good food. Wait, is that even a superhero? Or is that just a chef?" She buckled over from laughter, nearly spilling her dessert.

"You joke," I said. "Maybe that's his plan all along."

"Maybe," she added.

"Anyway, aside from that, I don't know that much about him. He's Filipino and super nice." I held up the cup. "As evidenced by the free food."

"All Filipinos are nice," said Ginessa. "You should try being one sometime. Maybe you'd have some friends."

THE FAMILY TREE PROJECT

By now, the anticipation of the first week of school had dwindled into the start of football season, homework, and, for Clint and Bart in particular, ruling the student body.

Clint sat a few rows behind me, his fellow football players surrounding the starting quarterback, as the teacher casually wrote something on the board.

It was my last class of the day: social studies.

"Okay, class," the teacher said, spinning on the ball of her foot. I read the message on the white board: 'Papers and Presentations!!! Topic: Your Family Heritage.'

Miss Francis, a petite woman who was dressed in a trendy charcoal jumpsuit with heels, pointed to the board behind her. She was a well-put-together woman. Her head was shaved in the back but her long bangs fell down the sides of her high cheekbones. She was my favorite teacher. She was so much different than the rest of them, mainly because she seemed hipper than the middle-aged teachers that waltzed into classrooms with their loafers and buttoned-down blouses and khakis. She was just different. It was like she understood teenagers.

"Does anyone know what's coming up soon?" she said, subtly gesturing to the board. "Hint, hint."

"The homecoming game?" Clint quipped.

"The homecoming dance?" Bart added.

A few kids laughed at the human sculptures' wisecracks.

"No," said the teacher matter-of-factly. She wasn't keen on enabling her students' behavior, considering she'd seen most of us in years prior at different times, which was another reason I liked her so much. "Research papers and presentations! Exciting, I know. I'm bringing this assignment up now because instead of having them all due at one time and going through days of presentations, they will be due on an ongoing basis."

I closed my eyes and exhaled deeply. There was a groan in the front of the room and an audible sigh in the back.

"So what does that mean?" she continued. "If you get it done next week, you can present it and you'll fulfill your requirement for the year. Just the same as if you don't get it done until the final week." She peered around the room for any questions or comments. There weren't any. "And although the paper and presentation won't be a large portion of your grade," she stressed, "I figured that you all would be more enticed to put a little more effort into it if we make it a little fun."

Fun? I thought. I couldn't imagine how anything pertaining to my family heritage would be fun.

Miss Francis glanced to the area where Clint and his fellow jocks were sitting.

"You're all going to vote on the best project. So, having said that—and I know we just started off the year—does anyone have any ideas?"

I opened my eyes. *Vote?* I thought, casually looking around the classroom for any engagement. But like before, nobody said a word.

Her gaze wandered around the classroom, zeroing in on the blank and disinterested faces. In all fairness, the school year was still ramping up, but given that this was our "big" project of senior year (at least for her), I could see why she was making it so important. A matter of life or death. Maybe she was getting tired of grading subpar work. Like she actually wanted what was best for her students.

Whatever the case, hearing "best project" got me excited. It was my chance to be the best at something before I graduated.

"Anybody?" asked Miss Francis.

One classmate cleared his throat, and another coughed, but for the most part, it was dead silent. As if nobody was interested.

"Just remember the parameters," she said. "It can be on anything that pertains to your family heritage."

My family heritage. I ground my teeth in frustration. The one thing I didn't want to write about. Winning would be harder than I thought.

She scanned the room once more, hoping the loose definition of her assignment would translate into volunteers interested in engaging. As if a flash mob of kids would suddenly jump from their seats, arms raised, with topics about their family in tow.

"Nothing?"

There were a couple more audible groans, this time by several kids at once, like we were all in the same position.

"Don't make this harder than it is," Miss Francis said. "Okay?"

Clint whispered something, loud enough for me to sneak a look. Why did I even bother? I died a little inside due to my own curiosity. But I knew why. It was Clint. His dominant personality was his superpower. Even I wanted to be like him, and I hated myself for it. Perhaps this project could get me to his level, if only for a day. Winning the most votes could take me from secret identity nerd to superhero Victor, just like that. I didn't have the looks or physique, so being extraordinary took more work. It was like my brown skin was Filipino kryptonite.

When my eyes caught his, Clint and the others were laughing amongst themselves. I couldn't hear the conversation until Clint, loud and boisterous, said for the entire class to hear, "I wonder if this presentation will be as epic as Victor's family tree project."

There it was.

The family tree project. I wondered how long it would take to come back around. Talk about exposing a secret that I wanted to keep hidden, that I was embarrassed about. The presentation had been a disaster.

Laughter unfurled around Clint like rolling thunder passing through the night. First it was the other football players, then kids in adjacent rows, and then the rest of the classroom, until each domino of laughter had fallen onto the class.

I stared into the desk, my forehead puckered, pulling my eyebrows together to the point my eyes were straining. I was horrified and embarrassed; my heart began to race and my palms started to sweat, all at the same time.

Miss Francis caught wind and quickly interrupted the teasing.

"All right everybody, that's enough."

The bell rang (thank God!), and the class was over. At once, kids shuffled out of the room in pairs and small groups. A few walked out alone.

"I'll see you next time," Miss Francis said to each classmate who passed. "And start thinking about your assignment! If you want me to look at a rough draft, I can do that as well."

I didn't move. Instead, I snuck a look as Clint and his crew sauntered out with their chins raised and their Cheshire Cat grins worn smug across their faces.

Miss Francis stared at them when they exited. I quickly jumped from my seat.

"Victor," she said. I froze, exhaling heavily as I slowly turned to address her. "Can you hang back for a moment?" Her lips twisted into an empathetic smile, and I could feel the sympathetic gesture brush upon me. I sat back down. "Do you want to talk about what just happened?"

"No," I whispered, my gaze drilling into the floor in front of me.

Before the air could suffocate me, she said, "I thought your family tree project was very interesting." I stayed silent, my eyes locking onto hers. "It was neat to see how much influence the Spanish had," she added, nodding to gain acceptance from me, "just in Filipino names alone."

"Thanks," I said under my breath.

"Have you ever thought about looking any of them up?" she asked. "Maybe they have some cool meanings." I shook my head. I hadn't. It had never even dawned on me to do so because I didn't have any interest in any further meaning. I just didn't want to talk about my family. Or my culture. Or anything that made me different.

Miss Francis fidgeted a tad, almost like she wanted to broach a subject she, too, had been avoiding.

"Victor," she said softly. "Are you comfortable doing an assignment based on your family with what happened to your parents?"

My eyes slowly drew to hers.

"I think so," I replied, even though I wasn't certain. But not for the same reasons that she suspected. I just didn't want to bring attention to anything related to my culture.

"Do you want to talk about it?" I shook my head and sulked back to my seat. "Okay. I can't excuse you from the assignment, but if you need help, I can certainly offer that."

There was some ruckus outside the classroom and Miss Francis turned to look. After her curiosity was satisfied, she returned to me.

"Don't mind Clint and Bart," she said. "I'm sure neither of them knows what you're going through. They're in their own little world, you know?"

They're on top of the world, I thought. And that was where I wanted to be. My lips tightened. *Was it that easy? To just deal with it?* I wondered.

"Well, I'm excited to see what you come up with this time around," said Miss Francis.

This time around, I thought. As sophomores, we completed a family tree project, and I didn't have Miss Francis again until now. Her classes revolved around humanities, and this year we were working on the family heritage project.

"I'm sure it will be just as interesting," she said.

A glimmer of hope barreled through me just from hearing the kind words that Miss Francis had said. Her optimism and compassion triggered me to life, kindling some ideas, which was why she was my favorite. She was always taking a little extra time to inspire.

"And remember," she began, "I'm here if you need anything from me."

I should have said something right then and there, but instead, I buried it inside, nodding without ever laying an eye on her.

"Now, let's get outta here," she said and winked. By now, the room was empty, quiet, and the day was ending—a ghost of a class.

Smiling, I stood from my desk, heaved my book bag up, and slung it over my shoulder. As I followed the teacher to the front of the room, Ginessa poked her head in.

"There you are." She turned to Miss Francis and greeted her with a phony, tight-lipped smile.

"Are you Victor's sister?" asked Miss Francis.

Ginessa politely nodded.

"Yes," she answered. "I'm Ginessa. It's my first year here."

"That's great. How are you liking things so far?"

"So far, so good."

The entire time I stayed silent, watching the exchange unfold before me.

"Well, it was very nice meeting you," Miss Francis said. Her eyes drifted subtly toward me. "I'll leave you two alone." She then left the classroom.

Ginessa turned to me.

"I've been waiting for you."

She seemed to have acclimated smoothly since becoming a high school student, but she still acted like she needed an escort from me, which I didn't get because she was tough as nails. I was certain she was doing little things like this for my benefit.

"How was class?" she asked.

"Sorry I didn't meet you. I got tied up talking to Miss Francis about my assignment."

"What's the assignment about?"

My eyes found the white board, and I quickly diverted my attention to the door so that she wouldn't follow my gaze.

"It's, uh, not due for a while," I answered and clenched my teeth.

I instantly wished I was the superhero Magik so I could teleport to another time to forget this moment ever happened.

THE FILIPINO BATCAVE

I wasn't scheduled to work, but Sir texted me that he needed me to run to his apartment for a stock of to-go containers that he forgot to bring earlier. I wasn't in the mood, but having the opportunity to see where he lived got me excited. I'd never been to a superhero's lair—I mean, house—so maybe I could see some cool things.

The directions seemed easy enough. The apartment was just off NW 10th and Hoyt, in some apartment building on the top floor. *Near a Starbucks and burrito shop,* the text read. *Can't miss it.*

But of course, I missed it. More than once. At one point, I'd circled the block numerous times in search of this magical burrito shop. It was like the Filipino Batcave in the middle of fifty Starbucks cafes.

I scratched my head when suddenly my phone buzzed.

Don't need after all, the text read. *I managed.*

Since I was only a few blocks from the cart, I decided to visit Sir. I had no trouble finding Filipino Feast. All you had to do was walk toward the river and sniff the air until it smelled like pancit.

Sir was closing when I arrived. The cart was immaculately clean, like it was never open for business. But the aroma lingered, and I instantly became hungry.

It was almost as if Sir had read my mind because as soon as we made eye contact, he asked, "Have you eaten?"

"I could eat," I said. "But let me pay—"

"Stop!" he said. "I always have leftovers to take home for dinner." He moved to the back of the cart and pulled out an aluminum tray container. He pulled up the creased ends of the lid and slid it off. A curlicue of smoke rose up to the ceiling.

"I have pancit and some lumpia," he said.

"I could smell it a block away," I said with an eager smile.

"Well then, let's eat."

I ran around to the back door of the cart and hopped in. Sir had already set up a small area on the prep counter for two plates.

There wasn't room to sit, so the two of us just stood over our meals. It was only slightly crowded but that didn't bother me. Spending time with him was totally worth it.

We dug in and it was quiet for the first several bites.

"Sorry I make you go on adventure," he said. "Turned out I had enough containers for just as many customers."

Sounds like magic.

"That happens," I said. I glanced around the cart, and a feeling of warmth fell over me. Being here made me comfortable, almost like I was at home.

"How was school?"

School.

I thought about telling him about the family heritage project but, like Ginessa, he was so proud and overjoyed about being Filipino. So, I simply shrugged.

"It was fine," I said. "Just ready to graduate."

"Then what?"

"I don't know. Work here, I guess."

He chuckled.

"I would love that, but you should begin thinking about what you want to do with life."

I'd never really thought about it. Just trying to get through high school was hard enough. Mom had broached the subject before she and Dad passed, but then afterward, I never thought more about my future. With their lives being cut short, would I even have one? The conversation fizzled as we finished our meals.

"You still hungry?" he asked.

I dismissed him with my hand.

"It was more than enough," I said. "Thank you."

"Let me clean up and we call it a day."

"Anything I can help with?"

"No, just need to throw trash away."

He tossed the empty plates and foil container into the garbage and pulled out the bag and tied it. There was a little bit of daylight left, and other cart owners were closing for the night as well. I stepped out the cart. Sir followed, closed the door, and locked it.

"What you doing now?" he asked. "Going home?"

"Was thinking about it," I said. "But I never found your place. Since I'm already down here, maybe you could show me where it is." I shrugged. "Just in case I have to run there again."

"Good idea," said Sir. He gestured to the community dumpster. "Let me throw this out first."

After tossing the trash out, he gestured for me to follow. The city was quieting after the rush hour commute. Only a few cars were on the road and the only pedestrians out and about were random joggers or restaurant-and shop-goers.

Along the short route, Sir said, "Maybe I give you wrong directions."

I checked my phone and repeated the text back to him. As I said the word "shop," we turned the corner and right in front of me was a Starbucks and burrito shop.

Everything looked familiar, like I was just there—because I was. Or was I?

"See?" he said, pointing to a customer exiting the burrito shop. "Can't miss it."

My mouth fell open, and Sir could tell that I was in shock.

"I swear I walked around this block a hundred times," I said. "I have no idea how I even missed it."

"Maybe you daydreaming," said Sir. "Or something on your mind."

Could be. What'd happened in school was weighing on me, mainly because I needed to find a topic about my family heritage that wasn't bland. I chalked it up to Sir's seemingly sixth sense. He was so keen about things.

We entered the apartment building and found our way to the elevator. The lobby and hallways were un-superhero-esque, as the paintings on the walls in the hallways were mass-produced and the carpet looked like a store's best seller, but that didn't deter me whatsoever.

I could hear synthesizer music as we got closer to his door.

Was there a party going on without him?

He unlocked the door, and unsurprisingly, it wasn't very big. The music increased in volume. It sounded like a music station randomly playing in the background, almost like a Pandora app or something was cycling mood music. I thought I would find the source, but I was distracted by the wall of tsinelas placed neatly on a shoe rack that started at the entryway of the door, went along the full wall of the living room, and ended just near the sliding glass door to the balcony.

There were dozens of them. All the same color and lined up perfectly.

I bent down to remove my shoes when suddenly there was a loud thump and the music turned off. The disruption caused me to look up and see that the television—which was at least ten feet away from us and seemingly the source of the music—had suddenly shut off. I turned to Sir who was adjusting one of his slippers like he'd either changed it or removed it.

"Did the music just turn off?" I asked even though I had my suspicions. The faded memory of the *oomcha, oomcha, oomcha* of the boomerang slipper incident darted through my mind.

"Oh," he said without missing a beat. "TV has . . . auto shutoff."

"Then what was that thump?" I asked. "It sounded like something hit it."

Dismissing me, Sir said, "I think that sound of app shutting down." He smiled wide and my superhero suspicions grew.

He held his pointer finger up.

"I almost forgot," said Sir. "Here is where I keep extra supplies for cart."

He quickly waltzed over to the closet and opened the door, stepping aside for me to look at the never-ending supply of containers, silverware, and napkins. Next to that was banana ketchup, soy sauce, and salt and pepper. All the essentials to keep his food cart running. Although small, the closet looked like a tunnel that went deep into the apartment building.

When I spotted the banana ketchup, I chuckled.

"My parents loved banana ketchup," I said.

"It staple in the Philippines because of all the bananas," said Sir. "Way more bananas than tomatoes."

I'd never thought about that. It was interesting to listen to him talk so casually about things in the Philippines as they related here in the States. Although my parents would mention these random tidbits of information, for some reason hearing them from Sir had a greater impact.

Sir closed the door.

"Go ahead and take a quick look around," he said.

My attention drifted from the ketchup to the slippers, both the ones he was wearing and the rows of tsinelas on the rack. I started investigating the rack.

"You have a lot of slippers," I said.

"Slippers big in Filipino culture too," answered Sir. "Tropical weather make feet sweaty. Plus, I do lot of walking." He nodded and then smiled.

"But why so many of them?"

"I buy in bulk," he replied. "But let me show you whole place."

"Okay, but . . ." I began, pointing toward the tsinelas.

"Those just smelly slippers."

There was only one bedroom and a small bathroom that branched off from the main room, which was comprised of a living room, a small kitchen, and a dinette area. I poked my head into the bedroom. It was just as disappointingly plain as the living room. I took a quick scan of the area but didn't notice anything unusual or that stood out.

Walking out of the room and into the narrow bathroom, I observed the shower, vanity, and small stackable washer and dryer unit. I spun around in a tight circle so I could exit. Sir definitely played the secret identity well. Nothing shouted superhero.

But then something caught my eye. On the back of the bathroom door, hanging on a towel hook, were three to four (I couldn't really tell because the cords made them appear like dozens of them) karaoke microphones.

I met Sir back in the dining area.

"What's with all the microphones?"

"Oh," he said without missing a beat. "I sing to music on app." He cleared his throat. "*La la laa la laaa.*"

I thought it was weird, but with the instrumental music playing when we entered, I dismissed it. Plus, Filipinos love karaoke.

Taking one last sweep of the apartment, I turned to Sir and said, "Nice place."

"Thanks," he replied. "This is where dreams begin."

I FELT LIKE DICK GRAYSON

During a work shift the next day, Sir was prepping a batch of siopao with pork. The steamed buns with filling were a hit at the food cart. At this point, the doughy pieces were flattened, and when he finished seasoning the pork with barbecue sauce, he looked at me.

"Wanna help?"

I glanced out the cart's window, and for the time being, there weren't any customers, just a couple with a beagle sitting on a picnic bench in a common area a few yards away. The beagle was sitting with perfect posture, silently begging its owners for some table scraps.

"Sure," I said and joined him in the kitchen.

"Not brain surgery, but there is art in folding so pork stays in," he said. "I do first one and then you."

Sir's fingertips gently grabbed the dough's edges. He was very delicate in his approach as he began twisting them together, his free fingers securing the pieces of pork so they didn't fall out. It looked like he was tying a shoe and adding his own flair to the knot. He finished the first one almost immediately.

"Now you," he said.

I tried one, but failed. Miserably. The dough loosened and Sir had to scrape off the pork and re-flatten the dough.

"Try again."

I did and this time I tore off the edges. The dough flaked off my fingertips and onto the counter.

"Like this," he said. He retrieved the loose ends, rerolled the dough, and then flattened it. He tied the edges together, and the result was an exact replica of the first one. "Now you."

Instantly, I felt like Dick Grayson being trained by Bruce Wayne. I just wasn't sure if there was a Gauntlet at the end of this. I couldn't imagine a scenario where I had to avoid Sir for any amount of time.

I tried another siopao. Two of the edges stuck, but the others I ripped off.

"Did you know Chinese introduce siopao to Philippines?" he asked. "Many Filipino dishes come from there."

"Which ones?"

By asking, I thought I could glean some superhero background from him. See what he enjoyed and figure out my theory about him. Maybe it related to some of the Asian superheroes out there, like Shang-Chi, Black Widow, and Jimmy Woo.

"Many kinds," he said. "Lumpia, pancit, hopia. Just to name a few."

"Have you had *congee*?" I asked.

I tried another bun. Same result as the last.

"You know congee?"

"That's what Shang-Chi eats at breakfast," I said. "In the Marvel movie."

Sir laughed.

"I not familiar."

"It's a superhero movie," I said.

Shaking his head, Sir replied, "Haven't seen it. But congee is Chinese. The Filipino version is *lugaw*. It's a rice porridge."

"Gotcha."

Finally, after a fifth try, I secured one. Although the knot looked janky, the filling stayed.

Sir patted my back.

"Not too bad," he said. "Just need practice." A voice from the window distracted us. We looked and Sir said, "Customer."

I greeted the boy and took his order: chicken adobo and some pancit. After relaying the meal to Sir, I practiced on the remaining pieces of dough, inserting filling until I had them all rolled into siopao.

Sir fulfilled his part of the order, then I rang the customer up and he left.

"Wow," said Sir, eyeing the finished siapao. "You do good job."

I thanked him.

"Not quite as fancy as yours," I said.

"I do this a long time. My fingers do all the work," he said. "Almost like it— "

"Magic?" I interjected.

"—automatic."

"Oh . . . because of how much practice you've had."

We moved to the window and looked out. Customers enjoyed meals, and for the rest of the night, it was quiet. Only a man here and a woman there ordered from the cart.

"If you really serious about working here after school," he said, "you should probably start to learn the food and heritage. Like learn it. Not just from what you see in movies."

There was that word again: heritage. It reminded me that I needed to come up with a topic.

Then Sir said, "It might not be bad idea to have sidekick."

ARE WE RELATED TO ROYALTY?

Another day passed.

I started to think more heavily about what to write about. I didn't want to endure another experience like I'd had with the family tree, so I figured I'd need something extraordinary, some amazing piece of family history. A scandal or lore perhaps? Anything to deflect my own Filipino heritage but that was indirectly tied to it.

Given the time we had to work on it, this was my opportunity to start this train on the right track. At this point—save for asking Ginessa, who, in my mind, would give me an earful—I opted for the path of least resistance to help with this assignment: Lola. I trudged toward the kitchen.

My relationship with Lola was similar to the one I had with Mom. Lola was just trying to figure out how to raise two teenagers again after years of her own daughter being out of the house. When she first moved in, it was almost like she'd forgotten how to raise kids. So when she suddenly had to take on parenthood again, I chose to stay out of the way so I wouldn't come across as burdensome. In my mind, I was easing her into things. I worked a part-time job and got good grades. That was all she needed to know.

I paused just outside her view, standing in the living room while she watched a rerun on some cable channel.

The show was *Jane the Virgin*, a cultural dramedy about a single grandmother raising her daughter and granddaughter. I watched for a second, noting the slight similarities to my own life, and thought of the best way to get her attention.

Clearing my throat—"ahem"—I softly made my presence known. Lola had a knack for always bringing up topics that I wasn't comfortable with. They were never anything I wanted to discuss, like why the DC movies continually lost the box office to the Marvel films? Could it be that the loveable superheroes I grew up with suddenly became too dark for my taste? I loved the classic Super Friends cartoons with their goofiness and puns.

But I guess since I'd developed this hands-off relationship (the same one I had with Mom), I could see why she was always thinking something was going on.

"Victor?" Lola's slight accent stressed the first syllable of my name. "Is that you?"

"Sorry," I replied, my eyes looping around the kitchen. "I was hoping you could help me with something."

Lola pushed the remote's power button and the screen turned black. The room became quiet. Her interest was piqued.

With raised eyebrows, she asked, "Is something wrong?"

"There's an assignment we were just given, and I don't know how to start it."

She looked me up and down. My body wilted.

"How can I help?"

"Well . . ." I began. "I have to write a paper about our family heritage."

Her lips softened into a gentle smile.

"Oh, that sounds like a wonderful subject," she said. "What have you come up with so far?"

"That's just it. I don't have anything to write about." I shrugged so hard my shoulders hurt. "Could you tell me something about the Philippines that, since I've never been, would *wow* the other kids? I don't know, like some neat history or some family mystery?" As I ended the question, I instantly recalled a similar conversation with Mom. "Are we related to royalty? Any hidden secrets I should know about?"

"Well, I can absolutely try to help," said Lola.

"I just don't want the same thing to happen as the last time."

"Ah, the family tree project," she said, nodding. "I heard all about that."

The infamous family tree project. Two. Years. Ago.

"Oh, you did?"

"I most certainly did," she said. "Your mother—God rest her soul—told me she spent the entire night filling it out for you. That it was due the next day and you needed to get a good grade."

I bit my lip and turned my head in shame.

"But I told her not to enable you, that you needed to take responsibility for learning about our culture." Lola's tone turned slightly serious as she said, "You're almost eighteen, and frankly, you've never taken an interest in your heritage. And I understand. You're a teen. Your mother was the same when she was your age.

Always out doing her own thing. But if you start caring about where you came from, maybe you could complete these assignments on your own."

"I understand," I said. My stomach twisted in guilt.

"But I'm definitely willing to help," she said.

"I just don't want it to be boring, you know?"

"Unfortunately, you don't come from anything other than a hardworking, immigrant family," said Lola.

"That's what I thought," I said. "Well . . . I guess it's not due for a while." I sulked.

"Victor," she said in a soft manner. "I think we both know that this has nothing to do with you not knowing what to write about." She leaned in close and looked me straight in the eyes. "If you can't accept that you are Filipino, then you'll be running from these things for the rest of your life. Your brown skin isn't going to lighten anytime soon."

How crushing. She was right, though. When I was younger, I'd tried to erase my skin with one of those pink pencil eraser blocks, but it only burned, and eventually I stopped.

"I know you have it in you," she encouraged.

Conceding to Lola's suspicions and my own self-awareness, I said, "I know I'm a horrible Filipino. It's just—"

"It's just nothing," she interjected. "I'm not sure your mother told you this. But did you know that she spent *hours* completing your assignment, even though she had to work early the next morning? She said that seeing those names brought back so many memories of her family, but she was so upset with you because the last thing she wanted to do that night was bail you out."

"I didn't know that last part."

"She'd just gotten home from work and prepared dinner for the family," said Lola. "Then her typically responsible son basically guilt-tripped her into doing an assignment last minute."

Wow, I thought. Mom was always so excited to talk about her family that she never conveyed that disappointment to me. And what did I do? I disappeared into my room without considering her feelings. I was such a douche. Now I was doing the same thing with Lola.

"Maybe this paper is a sign from your mother," Lola said. "She'd been wanting you to learn about where you come from—where *we* come from—for a long time."

Her eyes started to dampen, and she became quiet. Then she continued.

"Whenever she and your father would go home to the Philippines," said Lola, pausing to gather her breath, "she would tell them how proud they were of you and your sister. How she wanted to bring you and Ginessa home but couldn't because you couldn't miss school."

Home? Mom had asked if I'd wanted to go to the Philippines, but I'd never wanted to. I couldn't understand the language, and I didn't want to sit on that long of a flight. Home wasn't in the Philippines for me. Home was here: the States. Why didn't anyone get that? After a few times, she quit asking. Now, I was discovering that she made excuses for me. For all the times I didn't go. And wow, my family in the Philippines probably thought I was this busy kid who couldn't get away instead of the real reason: I was a horrible, horrible person who didn't give two damns about my family heritage.

Lola's head dropped to her chest.

The temperature in the room dropped, my knuckles whitening from the coldness, and when the silence became awkward, Lola said in a whisper, "I encourage you to try to look inside and figure out why you're like this. Do it for yourself. Try and find out why you hate yourself and why you hate being Filipino so much. Make your mother and father proud. Better yet, make yourself proud."

I sighed.

"But I have no idea what to write about," I said in a depressed tone.

If Mom was still around, she'd . . . My stomach hollowed into a nagging pain for multiple reasons, the main one being: How dare I wish she was alive for the sole purpose of bailing me out again? I bet Bruce Wayne didn't pity himself for losing his parents. *I'm just going to sit here in my tights. Woe is me.* No, he became Batman for Christ's sake!

The research paper had to be grand, amazing, some kind of fantastic that would divert the other kids' attention from the family tree debacle.

Beyond my immediate family—myself, Ginessa, and Lola—I had no idea who my relatives were. Even my father's name was on the verge of sounding foreign—Diosdado. And when my mother had filled in the rest of the names—Dalisay, Bayani, Bituin—they all looked funny and un-American. When Miss Francis looked to me for assistance in pronouncing the names, I was clueless as well. She asked about the origination of them and, nope, nothing came to me. Like why was she asking? I was American like everyone else. But that was when the class started laughing at me and my cluelessness.

It only added to my embarrassment. Here I was, a nerdy kid who got good grades in school totally botching a homework assignment. And, of course, it had to be about my family heritage. The one subject I *didn't* want attention on. Talk about exposing my vulnerabilities. It wouldn't have been so bad had word about the project not traveled across the school grounds in record time.

What I failed to realize was Diosdado, according to Lola, in Spanish, meant "God-given," which would have been cool enough to overcome the humiliation. *C'mon! God-given!*

Nonetheless, the family tree debacle scarred me. But finding out all this about Mom? That she secretly was frustrated about my project?

"I have an idea for what you can write about," she said. "But I'm sure you know what that is."

"I know, but—"

"Don't be ashamed of who you are," interrupted Lola. "Look at me. I speak with an accent. Do you think I care about what anyone says about me?"

She waited for a response from me that never came. Instead, I did nothing but stare, holding back emotions that I'd never felt before.

"For your information, I don't," she said.

My lips formed into a frown, and the combination of disappointment and failing at my own heritage hit me at once.

"Just let me know if you still need my assistance," said Lola. "I'm more than willing to help ensure you get a good grade. Otherwise, I'm sure you'll come up with something super."

She returned to her original business, pushing the remote's button to reawaken the television. Out barked a commercial for a local car dealership.

"Don't drop the ball on our huge savings!" a voiceover screamed. On the screen, a quarterback handed off the football to somebody out of the picture. Then he acted as if the ghost player scored a touchdown, shooting his arms into the air and staring into the camera with a wide smile. A computer-generated applause erupted from a fake crowd.

Focusing on the all-American teenager in the ad—Clint—I suddenly felt angry. The commercial had nearly ended when a disembodied voice said, "Our dealership has been family-owned for generations."

I ran to my room and slammed the door.

THIS CAN'T BE

A collection of memories flashed through my mind after Lola brought up the family tree project. Memories I'd been trying to forget.

Mom had just filled out the branches as accurately as she could, often referring to old photo albums she'd kept on the bookshelves. The branches didn't go too far back generationally, only up to her and Dad's great-great-grandparents, so I honestly didn't think it would take so long to complete. There was so much excitement on her face as she reminisced about times she'd had with her family. It was like she was in her own little world. A world that I wasn't a part of. A past life that only she knew.

She was so proud to tell me this story, saying that it brought up happy childhood memories. I could feel the joy spill out of her, but what did I do? I discounted it in a flash. I just wanted to get the project done. Honestly, I didn't care. My heritage took a backseat to, well, everything. Mostly because I didn't think of it as my heritage. I was born and raised in the Pacific Northwest, in the United States of America. I was a white, brown kid.

And then I presented the project. I walked up to the front of the room, my feet dragging like I'd been trudging through cartoon quicksand, and my classmates' eyes burned into me until they saw through me, their subtle comments muttered under their breaths in a language that only they'd known. When I stammered across the foreign sounding names of my family, none of whom I'd ever met or had even known about, and couldn't answer the follow-up questions, I finally asked to sit down.

All because I hadn't taken the time to review the project with Mom. I could have been the caring son and learned the pronunciations. I could have embraced her excitement. It would have shown that I was interested in our family, even though, deep down, I didn't care. It would have brought our relationship closer.

I could have brightened her day and my father's, who would have heard of the experience firsthand from Mom. I might have even escaped the presentation unscathed!

How would this have changed the course of my life?

I channeled my inner Doctor Strange so my superpowers would allow me to go back in time to navigate the situation to my liking.

I wasted no time on the assignment, excited to tell Mom about it when it was first assigned and how I couldn't wait to work on discovering our family members. Whenever there was someone we could assign to a branch, she told me his or her relationship to us. And if she didn't know, we researched together. I was genuinely intrigued with how this all pertained to me.

We spent hours over the course of days, weeks maybe, tracing our roots across the world, and even earning me extra credit.

After completing the tree, my knowledge of our family was expanded to the point that I actually wanted to visit them in the Philippines. Whether they were still alive or we would be finding their headstones, it didn't matter. It was about putting all the pieces together so I could see where I came from. Like an international treasure hunt.

Mom would have been so proud of me had this actually been the case. But unfortunately, I would never know how it could have altered the future.

My parents passed a year ago in a plane crash shortly after it had taken off from the Portland International Airport.

I had just arrived at school. Before the first period ended, the principal interrupted the class and pulled the teacher aside. The next thing I knew, I was being ushered to the front office. Lola, who had moved to the area to be closer to us, was there pacing in panic. My heart dropped into my stomach. It was difficult for her to speak. Instead, she pulled me into her and hugged me tighter than she ever had before.

"What's going on?"

Neither the principal nor my teacher had spoken a word. They stood uncertainly, almost frozen in a cocoon of ice like the victims of Mr. Freeze's freeze gun, incapable of emotion, not knowing what to say, or if they should say anything at all. It wasn't their place, I later realized.

I asked again. This time, more desperately.

"What's going on?"

My heart had never hurt so much. I felt shaky inside, and I couldn't control the movements of my limbs. It was like I was being electrocuted.

"They're gone," said Lola, holding in her tears enough to get the words out.

"What?"

"The plane they were on crashed." She released her grasp and looked at me. "There weren't any survivors."

"That can't be," I said.

I stared blankly at Lola, who was on the brink of losing it.

Mom and Dad were heading to the Philippines to visit family when an engine blew. The incident was all over television.

"We'll leave you two alone," said the principal, and he and the teacher left the office. I could hear faint voices from outside the room but none of the words were clear.

The last thing Dad told me was to take care of Ginessa while they were gone. This wasn't unusual; he said this every time they went home. My parents usually visited the Philippines for weeks at a time, as the trip alone was nearly equivalent to a day's length. It was the most beneficial use of my parents' time and money to make the most of it.

I would have seen them to the airport, even riding the train for the hour-long commute if they had asked, but they would never have dreamed of letting me skip class. School was on the top of their list of priorities, considering that both Mom and Dad immigrated to the States with hardly anything. The only thing on their mind was to get us kids a great education and achieve the American dream. That was probably the reason why Mom tried so hard on my family tree project. I'd had straight As in all my other classes, but this project could have brought my sociology grade down to a B, or worse.

Neither myself nor my parents made a fuss over their commute to the airport; instead, we said goodbye until next time. I'd never even imagined that there wouldn't be a next time, but it happened. I never saw my parents again.

My chin lowered, and as my eyes slowly began to tear up, the memory faded into the distance, bringing me back to the principal's office.

Suddenly, Lola burst into tears, her face reddening with each tear that fell down her cheek. I sniffled a few times, composing myself so I didn't lose it. I pulled her into me, and together we hugged until all of our strength left us and our bodies became numb.

We stayed like that for a while.

"Does Ginessa know?" I finally asked.

"Not yet," replied Lola. "I told you first because I need you to be the strong one when we do."

HE WAS A CHEF NINJA

I wasn't scheduled to work today, although it was a Saturday. Sir, like most Filipino elders, thought my education was important, so he usually gave me one weekend day off.

My plan was to start working on my assignment, but then my phone buzzed unexpectedly, the Superman theme ringtone piercing the air. It was a text message from Sir asking if I could work. Some event was happening nearby, and the influx of people greeted the food cart block by surprise.

He normally could handle a rush, so there must have been a lot of people. Whatever the case, it worked well for me.

I'll be there! I replied. I hustled out of my bedroom and down to the living room to tell Lola I got called into work. Then I headed out the door toward Filipino Feast.

I remembered I needed to stop by the ATM so I could pay back Sir for all the food he'd given to Ginessa and me. Even though Filipinos liked to feed each other, I didn't want to take advantage of Sir's kindness.

Sir reminded me of Dad, who I'd often disappointed because I wasn't interested in sports or music or any other extracurricular activities that could pad my college applications or yield scholarships—just comic books and action hero movies. I didn't want to continue that trend with someone like Sir. They were both roughly the same age and their voices were similar in tone and accent, but I felt like maybe he didn't want to judge me like my parents did. Sir made me feel safe for some reason, comfortable. I found solace in talking to him, despite not even knowing his real name. When I arrived, a semi-large gathering had crowded the space in front of the window.

Through the blank faces, I could see that Sir was entertaining the audience by juggling some frozen lumpia (it looked like four of them), spinning them quickly as he moved them from hand to hand. Just one giant showoff.

At one point, he flipped them higher and higher and spun around completely, catching them all simultaneously. Then he stopped and bowed.

Those witnessing the show applauded. Me? I did nothing more than stand frozen, amazed at Sir. He was one of the most interesting people I'd ever met.

He caught my gaze, pursed his lips, and smiled.

I greeted him, and we entered the cart from the rear entrance together.

"Lots of customers," he said. "They come from everywhere." He pointed down each street and in every direction. "But I had a short break in customer and wanted to attract more."

"Well, yeah," I chuckled. "You were out there putting on a good show."

He giggled.

"I need you to work the window while I make food," he said. "Just till we catch up."

I nodded, squeezed around Sir, and headed to the tiny space up front. Sir got busy in the back prepping for the new round of customers. His ploy had worked, and the customers had doubled due to the impressive performance. I swore he'd just quadrupled his sales for the day from doing nothing more than straight-up being super.

"What can I get you?" I asked.

A woman wearing a ball cap stepped up to the window. Her ponytail shot out the back, and the bill was curved just over her eyes.

"I gotta know," she said. "What was he juggling? Egg rolls?"

"Lumpia," I corrected her. "They're similar but not exactly the same. He could give you the entire history about each." I turned to get a better answer from Sir, but he was focused on making orders. Returning to the customer, I said, "Regardless, both are great with a sweet chili sauce. That's my favorite dipping sauce."

"I'll try that," said the woman. "One order of lumpia with that very sauce and an order of pork adobo."

When Sir finished her order, I asked him to explain the differences between lumpia and egg rolls. He was happy to.

"Look at the pastry," he said. "No egg in lumpia's wrapping. Typically made from just flour and water." He measured out a tiny cigar shape with his fingers, comparing the various sizes of each roll. "Egg rolls are thicker, heartier to eat."

I loved listening to him. Or maybe I loved being around him because . . . well . . . it was where I got an education in food and culture.

The woman thanked him and left.

Another person, this time a college student wearing a Portland State shirt, approached the window. And then another. I started collecting orders one by one until each person was satisfied.

While I waited for Sir to fulfill each order, I watched him work, then I boxed each dish accordingly. Suddenly, I was drawn back to thoughts about Dad.

The main difference between them was that Dad was introverted. He didn't draw attention to himself; rather, he was a reliable and modest friend, father, and man. Most people would describe him as a good guy and so caring, someone who would be there in a moment's notice. It was almost like Dad was Clark Kent and Sir was Superman: two different people, but also the same. And you never saw them in the same room.

Before my daydreams could take control of me, Sir shouted, "Order up!" He did this each time he finished a dish. He continued to slide each meal toward me, and I boxed and delivered them through the window to each customer. We never missed a beat.

He was a chef ninja, one hand sliding orders across the steel counter, while his other was tonging egg rolls out of the fryer. His foot, even though I couldn't see it from where I was standing, could have been unwrapping plastic silverware and napkins and combining them into one set to expedite each transaction. He was that good! I honestly didn't know how he managed to stay so calm. Although the thought of his feet against silverware triggered my gag reflex, he was easily the coolest person I'd ever met.

That got me thinking. How in the world could he possibly fulfill all these orders in such a short time and not screw anything up? Since, in my mind, he clearly was a superhero, I started focusing on where his potential powers could come from.

Sir's motions increased as the orders multiplied, his hands shuffling and rotating faster and faster. I swore he duplicated himself like Multiple Man, creating perfect copies of himself to satisfy his customers. One Sir wasn't enough, so my eyes were seeing four of them. Now five. Oh my God, now eight!

"Order up!" he yelled again, repeating the process.

Shaking my head, I realized I had fallen into dreamland again. I grabbed the meal and frantically ensured that each order went to the correct person while orchestrating a system where I didn't screw up counting out change for those rare customers that still paid with cash. It was crazy!

When the lunch frenzy finally died down, Sir looked at me and nodded.

"Great job," he said. "Teamwork make dream work."

Watching him fulfill orders to perfection only added to the mystery surrounding him.

Then he asked, "Have you eaten?" He spun around, eyeing a fresh batch of lumpia. I followed Sir's gaze, the smell of fried wrapping hitting me hard. Peanut oil sizzled in the background. "Also have pancit." He reached for a paper plate, but I stopped him.

"Don't do that," I said. "You can't keep giving me free food. How will you make money?" I reached for the pocket where the money from the ATM was and started to pull it out. "I have money to pay for the dinner you spotted me and Ginessa the other day."

"I told you not to worry about it. Filipinos always feed each other," said Sir as he returned the plate to its proper location. "It's in our blood." I chuckled. "Plus, you saved my butt today. You get free meal bonus."

He was right on all accounts. Filipinos always *did* feed one another. It was just a Filipino thing. A way to bring us together.

"Deal!" I said. "But only on days I'm called in because you already give me a generous discount on my normal workday."

Come to think of it, Lola was continuously offering food to my classmates, just like my parents used to do with our friends in the neighborhood. And Ginessa was deciding on what food dish to make for the picnic. It was always food.

Food. <3
Food. <3 <3
Food. <3 <3 <3

Once, Lola wanted me to bring to-go plates to school. She'd wrapped barbecue shish kebabs in aluminum foil and kept leaving them by my backpack, but I never took them. Instead, I placed them in the fridge to eat later. After a few times, she finally stopped. Just like Mom asking me to visit the Philippines. She never said a word, as if I could choose for myself, and I always seemed to choose badly.

Then it hit me.

Maybe if I brought Clint and Bart some Filipino food when we'd first met, we'd be best buds. My heart suddenly screeched to a halt. Oh my God. What if my one opportunity to exist at school with the popular crowd was completely under my nose? Use my Filipino heritage as a positive instead of shying away from it. I mean, look at Filipino Feast and how popular it was. Could I have been one of the cool kids simply by bringing in egg rolls and adobo? Like an appetizer food dealer of sorts secretly selling egg rolls from the inside of my coat jacket.

"What do you want? Lumpia? I've got veggie ones and pork ones. How about hopia? There's ube, Nutella, red bean, or yellow mungo. Whatever you want, I'm your man."

Who was I kidding? How dumb did this sound? It didn't matter, I was on a roll! Sir could be the leader of the Filipino food empire, and I could be his partner! His sidekick! We could take this food cart on the road!

I suddenly pictured us in matching tights with capes that complemented each other: not the same color, but definitely hues that worked well together. We wouldn't want to look like one of those couples who wore the same sweater. That would be weird. We were superheroes who peddled lumpia for Christ's sake, not an embarrassing TikTok couple.

As my mind went from being blown to nothing short of ridiculousness, Sir said, "Victor?"

I shook my head, erasing the situational comedy brewing within, and a faint smirk flashed across my face.

A herd of customers suddenly formed in front of us. Whatever event that was happening must have ended. Time for the early dinner crowd.

Sir winked and returned to his post at the fryer and stovetop.

"It's go time."

THE LASSO OF TRUTH

"Who's first?" I asked.

A patron ordered a halo-halo, and as I turned to check if there were still pieces of flan, a man off to the side swooped in and swiped the plastic tip jar that was converted from a small Miracle Whip jar.

The jar sat on the farthest side of the window ledge, away from the action but close enough for customers to toss in donations or change they'd received after paying. I honestly didn't think Sir wanted us to get any tips, but maybe a customer or adjacent cart owner convinced him that it was a good idea.

I wouldn't have noticed had it not been for our customers, one of whom screamed at the top of his lungs at the thief.

"Hey!" the customer yelled. His voice was like a siren relaying a nearby tornado—all I thought was to take cover immediately. "That guy just stole the tip jar!" Then he pointed. Sir and I ran to the window and followed the man's finger toward the crook.

"Aren't you going to do something?" I asked Sir, thinking immediately of the incident with one of the boomerang tsinelas.

Sir eyed me. His gaze then turned toward the crowd of patrons in front of us. He paused for a moment.

"Nothing I can do about it," he said. "He got away."

"He got away?"

I couldn't believe what I was hearing, Sir just acting casual about his tip jar getting stolen. Why couldn't he whip out his slipper to stop him like he did with the purse thief? I *knew* I hadn't hallucinated it because after the incident the other witnesses were chatting in disbelief about what they'd seen. Sir was acting as cool as the halo-halo that he served. Plus, I swore he turned that television off with his slipper. Why was he trying to hide this power?

What could I do to figure this out? *Aha!* My imagination took hold of me.

Attached to my belt was the Lasso of Truth. It was a weapon that Wonder Woman deployed onto criminals to extract the truth from them.

I twirled it over my head, flung it around Sir, and tightened it so that the lariat's magic could reveal the truth. He instantly fell into a hypnotic trance and began confessing his superpowers.

His life.

His backstory.

"When I was younger, a small Sir growing up in small mobile home composed of other Sirs and Madams who had no money or resources but had big ambition, I had to whip up meals with random ingredients found in trailer in order to survive. One time I make mean macaroni and cheese with rubber bands and mayonnaise. It turned out nasty but I ate it every afternoon with a milkshake I drank through a salami straw. Survival was key. And if I could learn to love rubber bands and mayo, I could learn to achieve anything. Chef Gonzales led group of eight of us. He found us, one by one, in various parts of world, trading our caregivers' magical pieces of clothing for a chance to teach us the culinary arts. Our caregivers were poor so trading us was best thing to do. For them and for us. Chef taught us one important lesson: Give man lumpia, he eat for a day. Teach man to cook lumpia, and if he Filipino, then he feed every person he meets for rest of life. What I didn't know was that Chef made me prize student. He taught me important lessons. Most important one was not be greedy. Second most important lesson was be thankful for health. And third most important lesson was sharing the wealth. My wealth was food. I worked years perfecting my craft and once I became master, Chef Gonzales gave me prize possessions—my foam tsinelas. It was there I became me: Sensei Tsinelas."

"I knew it!" I tightened the lasso.

A gust of wind suddenly smacked my cheek.

"Stop it!" it said, bringing me back to reality.

Sir was staring at me. He wasn't even paying attention to the thief.

"What about your tsinelas?" I asked.

"What you mean?" he said as he walked back to the kitchen.

A woman with glasses approached the window. Her smile was inviting, and her eyes told us one thing—she wanted Filipino food. She placed her order: pancit *bihon*.

"The last time—"

"What you want in your pancit?" he said to the customer in line, ignoring me to the point that I stopped mid-sentence.

I stood in a daze, still baffled by what was happening. I stayed like that until Sir elbowed me.

"Get back to work," he said, returning to his position in the back of the cart. He turned to the woman and said, "Victor take care of you."

The woman was just as confused as I was.

"Do you want to call the police or something?" she asked me.

I didn't know how to respond, so I shrugged.

"I guess we'll talk about it later," I said. "He's being really weird right now."

The woman subtly nodded and paid for her meal.

Once we got the patrons fed and the crowd finally cleared, I said to Sir, "Why did you do something before but not now?"

"What I do before?"

"The slipper!" I stressed and acted out the motion with my sneaker, fake-whipping it out into the air, retrieving it, spinning it in the air like a pistol-wielding outlaw after a shootout, and finally placing it back on my foot. "Remember?"

Sir's eyebrows furrowed. He looked down at his tsinelas as if they were aliens of some sort. I could tell that he was thinking of something—something that was conflicting inside—almost as if he'd fallen under a spell and his slipper had a mind of its own.

Shaking his head, he said, "Oh, that was nothing. Luck." Then he attempted to look busy by searching randomly in the food cart, picking up various utensils or supplies and examining them for quality. At one point, he sniffed the air as if something was burning, but this was Sir. Nothing was burning. His food was always cooked to perfection. To me, he was a chef-ninja/apparent slipper-wielding superhero.

"I'm pretty sure it was *not* nothing," I said in total disbelief. "It looked like you knew what you were doing. You're like a superhero!"

"No, it was nothing," Sir dismissed. "And I'm definitely not a superhero."

My jaw dropped. "You really don't want to talk about this?"

"Money isn't everything," said Sir—a mantra I'd heard before.

"But why not stop him?" I pleaded. "He took our tips."

"Victor," he said. "Crime is for the police to solve. Not me. Plus, no one hurt."

My mouth dramatically opened, and I stared in disbelief.

"Like before, you could have done something," I said. "You were a superhero."

Sir looked me straight in the eyes and said, "Victor, there no such thing as superheroes."

CHIHUAHUA THROW?

I wasn't certain why Sir opted to avoid confrontation with the tip jar bandit. I mean, the tips in the jar weren't much, maybe around fifty bucks, but Sir's mythical image became tarnished. If he would have foiled the robbery and salvaged his tips with all those in attendance, he would have to multiply himself tenfold just to keep up with the increased popularity. It just didn't make sense.

I'd discussed this with another customer who'd also thought it was strange that Sir would just let the tips go. He chalked it up to the amount not being worth the hassle, but for some reason, I couldn't get over it.

Later, I'd tried googling the slipper throw after I'd witnessed it, but I couldn't find anything. Part of me thought it was because my search was too vague. So, I stopped trying. But now, I was just plain bothered.

Someone had to have filmed it even though there weren't that many people around. Right?

I decided to search for evidence yet again, something to reinforce my belief that I wasn't crazy. That'd I'd seen it. That it was real. There was so much stuff on the internet it would take forever. But I had to try.

    🔍 "tsinelas throw"

Google returned a question: Did you mean chihuahua throw? The image of people hurling small dogs crossed my mind, and the visual disgusted me. So, I tried again.

    🔍 "July 29"
       "slipper throw"
       "Portland"
       "food cart"
       "Filipino"

Like before, the results were too vague.

🔍 "Filipino Feast"
"slipper"
"foiled robbery"
"July"

Nothing.
Filipino food, cart owner, throw slipper, foiled robbery?
Nothing.
Search.
Nothing.
Search.
Then, a video surfaced. A grainy, shaky, and poorly shot clip. From the still frame, the scene appeared right. All the surroundings seemed good. They looked like food carts. Could it be?

At this point, the video had already gained thousands of hits. Although the scene looked familiar, when I watched the footage closely, it wasn't the slipper throw after all.

In between the fuzzy pixels was Sir juggling egg rolls. A semi-large crowd gathered around him, with one spectator tossing in Mahjong tongs while Sir interchanged the rolls and tiles.

The crowd was totally into it. Whoever was manning the faraway camera must have spotted it during a shift and joined in on the fascination like everybody else. From this angle, it was almost as if I was that person.

The video played out, and I continued my search.

🔍 "boomerang"
"slipper"
"downtown"
"PDX"

A video surfaced titled "Portland Vigilante Appears at Protests." It looked semi-professional, like a blogger for an independent publication had filmed it to document the event. As the ads played, I read the description beneath the clip.

"On a cool fall day in October 2011, around ten thousand protestors descended onto Pioneer Square to march against corporate greed and the government bailout of businesses during the Great Recession. It was inspired by the Occupy Wall Street movement and was properly

dubbed Occupy Portland. Many residents had attended to bring awareness to economic inequality.

The march was peaceful until it wasn't. A few rowdy protestors began to cause a ruckus and one of them began aggressively bumping into another person's back.

The other person was the vigilante."

Your video will continue after this 60 second ad.

After the longest minute I ever experienced, I was about to see what I was possibly—hopefully—searching for: proof that Sir was a superhero.

The clip panned out over the square again. Rows and rows of protestors were milling around for the same cause. Then, it zoomed back in on the ruckus, close enough to make out what happened, but far away enough that faces could not be identified—just blurred heads and warped facial features that appeared as if they were melting. The blogger narrated the video like a reporter on assignment.

As we now know, the one-percenter plants (agents used to cause disruption to a peaceful protest) snaked through the chanting sounds of protestors, pushing and shoving their way, distressing and agitating the crowd. Annoyed but not bothered enough to act, the unknown vigilante inched his body away from the group. He stepped far enough to assess what was going on. But when he saw the hooligans begin harassing innocent and peaceful protestors, he could no longer standby.

We see the vigilante reach down for something. Like a shoe or sandal. It was later reported by an anonymous eyewitness that the object was, of all things, a slipper! The vigilante zeroed in on half a dozen irritants and took aim.

The vigilante hurled the slipper at the closest member. The slipper struck his head with a loud thud, suspended in midair, pelted the next person's forehead (SMACK!), rose to the sky a few feet, spun several times, hit the next goon in line's neck ("Ow!"), made a sharp turn toward the riverfront, slapped the next man's cheek ("What the?"), whistled around to the agitator next to him, struck the final person's nose ("Oy!"), and then curled back around until the slipper was back in the vigilante's hand. The scene looked like a rock skipping on the Willamette, making contact several times, only to return as if it ricocheted off a bank.

The clip ended and suddenly, I had the keywords I was hoping for: "Occupy Portland" "vigilante" "slipper".

The results displayed a whole new world. Portland had suddenly become Gotham. Multiple posts pertaining to it, all referencing the same vigilante video. There were Batman-style memes shouting "*BAM!*" and "*KAPOW!*" Random blog posts. All for your reading appetite. All just a few clicks away.

And they all pointed to one claim—a vigilante in Portland was fighting crime with a slipper.

I knew it! This had to be Sir!

I clicked through the search results with a hearty ambition, sitting in secrecy with a dim computer light exposing the contents.

There were past articles written by bloggers, journalists, and admirers—the most recent feature nearly five years prior.

One saying Sir was what Portland needed at the time. The people's vigilante.

Most of the stories were positive in nature, until there was one that wasn't. It was a statement released by the city of Portland's website saying that a man was out in the city performing unexplainable acts. Some vigilante who the police hadn't been able to identify, a person who the city, not the people, believed was doing more harm than good.

Most publications in the area reported the press release, tying the statement to the Occupy Portland video. This action was thought to repress the situation, but the top comment said it all:

"If you witnessed the slipper throw like I had, you would agree that it was downright magical."

Many commenters agreed even though the press release was specific: leave the crime fighting to the police.

BAM! KAPOW!

Even though a couple days had passed, the discovery was still fresh in my mind. A slipper throwing vigilante. A.k.a. superhero! A.k.a. Sensei Tsinelas!

What could I say? I knew it!

I didn't mention the subject again to Sir since he was adamant about superheroes not existing. Or anyone for that matter. Nobody believed in superheroes like I did. Anyway, what good would it have done? The only person who didn't want the police to stop crime, it seemed, was me.

So instead, I rewatched the video of the Occupy Portland event for the umpteenth time—while I was brushing my teeth, showering (yes, my hand was out of the water's way), and styling my hair—largely because I worried that my obsession was a dream and I wanted to ensure that the event had occurred. When the video popped up on the screen, I knew it was real—all five glorious minutes of it.

Slipping into clothes, I entered the kitchen to find Lola prepping some food.

She was sitting at the small table, mixing cut-up pork pieces to toss into the large bowl in front of her. She was making barbecue pork shish kebabs. It was a fan favorite, no doubt. I could eat a hundred of them in one sitting.

I inhaled deeply.

"Smells delicious," I said in a sing-song manner. "Pork kebabs?" Slowly inhaling the aroma of the soy sauce fused mix, my eyes closed in chorus. I raised my palms in front of me, pushing the scent to my nose so that I could get the full effect. I'd practiced this motion over and over, watching myself in the mirror to see if I looked convincing.

Lola, noticing my newly positive attitude, raised her brows in good humor, causing a row of wrinkles to crisscross her forehead like a breakdancer's arms doing the robot.

"You're in a good mood," she said.

"What's not to feel good about?" I chimed. "I'm alive, I'm healthy, I'm—"

"—slightly amused," she said, her lips curving in a smile. Suddenly, her eyes narrowed in on me. "A few nights ago, you were freaking out about your assignment." Her lip curled. "And then you hide out in your room for days it seems, and now this morning, you're walking around like you don't have a care in the world. Something happened in between then and now. So, what changed? What could possibly have happened in that amount of time?" She then walked to the sink to wash her hands.

What could possibly have changed? *BAM! KAPOW!* rang through my head.

Walking back to the table, she plunged her hand into the bowl and started massaging the meat with the sauce. Scattered around her were various ingredients—soy sauce, garlic, vinegar, banana ketchup, black pepper, barbecue sauce, and a two-liter bottle of Sprite. A bunch of skewers were soaking in water, waiting for the pork pieces.

Lola breathed in the marinating meat, her brows contracting slightly.

"A little more pepper please?" she asked since her hands were covered in sauce.

I grabbed the pepper and asked, "How much do I put in?"

"Don't worry. Just start adding and I'll tell you when to stop." After a few churns of the pepper grinder, Lola told me to stop. She mixed the newly added pepper in and said, "See how the pepper is evenly dispersed but there isn't too much?"

"No, not at all."

She chuckled.

"Well," Lola said, "you will the more you help, and you should learn since you love these so much!"

My mind went to my training session with Sir and the siopaos. I didn't even have to smile at the memory. I was already ecstatic.

"Now, I'm waiting," said Lola. "Tell me why you're so happy."

Here goes nothing.

"Do you know any Filipinos who own a food cart in downtown? The big food cart block on 3rd Avenue?"

Lola continued mixing.

Craning toward me, and with a lost expression, she said, "Could you elaborate? There are a lot of food carts in Portland. Plus, there are a lot of Filipinos. Just look at the Filipino-American Association alone. There are a thousand or so members." Her chin raised. "Why are you asking? Typically, you have zero care about the Philippines."

I ignored the comment and instead launched into the monologue.

"The cart that I work at . . . the owner—"

Lola's necked jerked back.

"Wait," she said. "I know your boss. He sent a ton of food home with you and your sister the other day." Then she paused, a faraway look in her eyes. "Well, I don't know him, know him, but I have met him before. Some of the association members were passing out flyers to promote membership and his business was one we'd approached." She smiled. "He seemed very nice. And he owns one of the better Filipino food carts. He never shows up to any events, though."

"The best food cart," I said.

"You never really talk about him or anything since . . ." Her voice trailed off for a moment. "Honestly though, I can't really say I could pick him out of a lineup."

"Well, he's balding, hair cut short on his sides, round face, pot belly." Lost in thought, my gaze drifted toward the ceiling. Now that I'd thought about it, Sir's physicality was very un-superhero-like. The perfect secret identity. "He kind of reminds me of Dad a little. Not physically, just something about him." A soft smile formed on my mouth as a memory of Dad passed through my mind.

Dad was always there for us kids and never once let us down. He was so giving, like Sir. One time, during grade school, I'd forgotten to bring my birthday treat. I fretted about it, believing my classmates would be mad at me for not bringing a treat even though it was my birthday. Anyway, the teacher called Dad at work, and within an hour, he'd left his office and hand delivered the cupcakes and juice to class. All so I wouldn't feel uncomfortable. All so I wouldn't be embarrassed. All so the other kids would accept me.

Pursing her lips, Lola shook her head.

"Like I said, I've met him," she replied. "But your description could apply to a lot of people. Although, I will say that I'm glad he reminds you of your father. You can find someone to relate to. Maybe even talk to?"

"I've always thought he was interesting," I said. "And the other night, I discovered the most incredible thing about him."

"Yeah?" she replied eagerly.

"I've never seen anything like it!"

Whipping out my cell phone, I pulled up the video of the protest and held it up for Lola, who was now letting the meat rest, to view. She watched with curiosity.

When the part came where the vigilante hurled the slipper into the crowd, Lola's smile broadened, and her eyes flashed with the same gleam that the witness had shared.

"After this, I'd definitely like to get to know him better," Lola said as she pulled back from the phone and once again concentrated on her task. "But why do you think that's him?" She looked at me with a quizzical expression.

I relayed the story about the would-be purse napper if not for Sir. I mean, I wasn't one hundred percent certain, but it had to be! I had convinced myself ever since I'd discovered the video.

"I'm thinking about writing about him," I said with giddiness, rushing out the words.

"Writing about your boss?"

"Yeah," I replied. "Remember, you said that you were sure I would think of something super? Filipino. Super. Superhero. SuperFilipHero! Eh?"

"Mm hmm..."

"I'm going to use this video, along with the incident I witnessed, for the research paper on my family heritage. Bring his legacy to glory while helping my own cause!"

I could see the paper forming in my head as I spoke, the words practically writing themselves with the right combination of diction and syntax. Winning best project was in the bag.

"Don't you think that's a great idea?" I asked.

Lola hesitated. A concerned expression slowly formed across her face. She cocked her head.

"Uh," she slurred, "I thought your assignment had to be about *family* heritage? As in *your* family. Something more about the Dela Cruz name." She then skewered pieces of marinated pork butt. When there were enough bits of meat on each stick, she laid them side by side on a sheet of aluminum foil. "And what about your boss? Have you talked to him about this?"

"He's Filipino. Plus, he's fine. We're all family."

Lola's chin dropped toward her chest. She gave a disapproving look that caused me to take a step backward.

"I mean, he *could* be related, right?" My heart fluttered with insecurity. I could feel Lola's disapproval pouncing on me. She crinkled her eyes and her lips closed tightly.

"He may not be related, but he *is* Filipino," I stammered, scrounging my mind for the right thing to say. "And a superhero to boot!" But really it just came out long-winded. "And Ginessa said that all Filipinos are related. That's how I got here."

Lola wore a sour expression, but all I could think about was winning the best project and riding off into graduation as a cool kid.

"Or maybe you could write about your parents?" she said. "I think that would be more realistic."

"Besides," I explained, ignoring her attempt to persuade me once again. "This will get me started on learning about my family heritage." My heart was in a dead-on sprint. "And isn't that what's important?"

Lola raised one eyebrow with suspicion. Instantly, I saw Mom. Then I saw Ginessa.

"I don't think writing about a chef—"

"Superhero," I interjected.

Lola cleared her throat.

"Victor," she softly uttered, "I know superheroes are important to you and they somehow get you through what happened. Losing your parents is very traumatic. Trust me, I lost family too, but I don't think writing about someone who has nothing to do with our family other than being Filipino is the best thing to do. Plus, I'm not even sure that's him."

"Who else could it be?"

She winced.

"It could be anyone," she answered. Lola placed her palm on my forearm. "Are you sure that you're not trying too hard?"

"I don't think so," I rattled out, yanking my arm out from under her. But she wasn't buying it.

"Listen," said Lola. "You're almost a grown-up, so I'm not going to tell you what to do because you've always gotten good grades and have, for the most part, been a good student."

Most part? I thought. *Oh.* Then I realized she was referring to the family tree project, and now this.

"So, whatever you need to do to justify your decision is on you," continued Lola. "Just remember, your family heritage, no matter how boring or embarrassing, is your family heritage. You can't change it. You can't make it up. It was how you were raised. And all you can do is embrace it."

She skewered a few more sticks and placed them next to the rest. The muscles around my mouth tensed and I felt slightly ashamed.

"To me, making something up to be accepted would be more embarrassing than the truth," she said, lowering her head, her eyes now staring directly into my soul. It was too much. My gaze turned downward, and I shuddered. "But it's nice to see you so enthusiastic about learning about your heritage." Her eyes glanced over my phone. "Even though I don't think it's him."

Before I could respond, Ginessa appeared.

I thought about showing the clip to Ginessa, but I wasn't prepared for anymore disappointment.

"Ready?" She had her school bag in hand and her hair was styled as usual: pulled back into a ponytail, bangs down her forehead. She dressed in a different type of baro't saya combination, this one a tad more fluorescent in color.

She slung the backpack around her shoulder and turned to Lola.

"I'm thinking about making a flan for the picnic. But before I commit it to the spreadsheet, will you help me if I need it? I want to make it perfect."

Lola smiled. "Of course I will."

"Thanks," said Ginessa. "I'll probably hang out with some friends tonight, so maybe tomorrow."

Lola's eyes flitted in my direction.

"It's nice to see you so interested in your heritage because you *want* to be," she said. The stare hit hard. "And *not* because you feel pressured to. Or because you have something to prove."

BRIGHT YELLOW OPAL APPLE

Later that afternoon in the cafeteria, I carried a tray full of the day's hot lunch—spaghetti and meatballs, green beans, corn bread, and a glass of water. It was the school's Italian meal and one of my favorite dishes that was offered. Usually, the lunch options tasted like carboard or were stale.

The cafeteria was at near capacity, with barely a scattering of empty seats. Conversation filled the air, chitchat floating among the student body, but I didn't hear any of it. I surveyed the entire space, but I didn't see Ginessa. Most of the time she was here before me, so I found myself playing this game of spotting her in the sea of faces. I only wished I had eyesight like the Avenger Hawkeye who had superhuman vision like a bird of prey.

I took a quick peek at my phone and saw that she'd texted me. I must have been zoned out because I didn't feel the vibration.

Outside by big tree near bike racks, the text read. *2 full in there.*

The path to the door was a straight shot, except that I had to pass the table of football players to the right. Most notably, Clint. I could have—make that should have—walked around the perimeter, away from the table, and took the long way out. But for some reason, I didn't. I tempted danger with the thought that a superhero loomed over my existence. Like a slipper would somehow whir through the cafeteria doors, zigzag through the table of heads, and knock the football players over.

I smiled at the thought of possessing such superpowers. Like having a slipper-silhouetted light similar to the Bat Signal or something at my disposal.

Reaching the table of players, Clint's presence willed my attention, pulling my gaze over to him. This time, however, I ignored him and beelined for the exit.

When I exited the school, the feeling of liberation brushed over me. I suddenly felt destressed, and I walked down the pavement to the grassy area where Ginessa was sitting. Her book bag was sitting upright against the tree trunk.

I was almost there when a voice behind me shouted, "What'd you buy me for lunch?"

Clint.

His voice sent a jolt of fear through me but for some reason (why did I keep doing this?), I turned.

Clint was with his crew. His right-hand man, Bart, stood by his side.

An empty chocolate milk carton buzzed by my face. I crouched instinctively, and the tray that I was holding tottered to the side, nearly causing a slow landslide of food to come crashing down. I flexed my arm, leveling out the tray. The blob of spaghetti slid back to the center of the plate and a few pieces of green beans shifted on top of each other.

In my head, I imagined having superhuman strength and holding a bridge upright as cars frantically crossed it after an earthquake knocked down its pillars. My body was flying underneath it and my stretched arms held up the span of the platform until the final car passed over.

When I blinked, my plate of food was resting still.

Exhaling like I was blowing out a large campfire, I whispered, "Phew."

A sense of relief poured over me, a dimpled grin subtly forming on my face. For some reason, I felt as if my instincts had sharpened by discovering Sensei. Like energy was coursing through my veins, giving me superpowers. There was no way I would have dodged embarrassment had I been mild-mannered Victor.

But then I saw something bright yellow and blurry in my peripheral flying toward me. I turned my head and there it was: an Opal apple.

The color reminded me of the yellow sun of Earth, which gave Superman his powers. Instantly, I ducked and the apple hurled over my head. I thought for one moment that my theory about gaining power from the sun was true, but my arms suddenly shot up from the quick motion. The tray of food catapulted on top of me. Marinara sauce splattered my face, speckling a pointillism art piece that could go for millions at auction. Noodles fell on my head.

In an instant, Clint's tight group burst into laughter. Soon, most of the kids loitering around were joining in on the scorn. It was the hey-they're-not-making-fun-of-us-for-once-so-let's-join-in-while-we-can reaction.

I, however, closed my eyes, and immediately the noise disappeared. I was, once again, alone in my thoughts. I brought myself back to my fortress of solitude. I'd decorated my room to my liking. It was one of the things Mom and Dad encouraged me to do. To express myself. All the things that made me who I was, I observed closely. Almost as if I was attending an exhibit about myself, how I was unique and special and not the loser or nerdy kid that everyone thought I was.

The brief detour from reality helped a tad, but soon I was jolted back when the laughter increased. The reality was, the Green Lantern shirt I was wearing was now stained with a creamy orange. It would take some stain remover to get the color back to its superhero glory. I stood upright and dropped the tray to the ground, now covered in my own lunch. I stomped forward toward Ginessa.

A wave of mockery greeted me with every step—laughter, pointing, teasing—until my racing heartbeat and grinding teeth drowned out the noise.

Ginessa pushed out a sympathetic smile when I reached her. She scooched over to make room for me. I shook out my shirt for any loose strands of spaghetti and then sat down in front of her. Ginessa witnessing all this was bad enough but sadly she was sitting with two friends she'd met the first day.

"Have you two met my brother?" she asked her friends.

"Not formally," one of the girls said. She had a slight underbite when she talked. "But I've seen you around."

"This is Elena," said Ginessa, gesturing to the girl who'd just spoken. "And that's Denise."

Denise greeted me with a closed-lip smile, and I could tell she was speechless. Unlike Elena, her face was round, and her hair fell just above her shoulders.

Ginessa stared at me.

"I don't want to talk about it," I said.

I couldn't look her in the eyes, so my gaze darted to the grass. Although I wasn't looking directly at Ginessa, I could tell that she was staring over at Clint. Elena and Denise just kept to themselves, not knowing how to respond. I lifted my chin and followed her gaze.

Clint and his band of jocks were choking on laughter.

She turned to address me, almost mother-like. Mama bear mode, to be precise.

"Are you going to do anything about it?"

Shaking my head, I said in a soft voice, "No."

Ginessa stood.

"Fine," she said. "Then I will."

I sprang up in a panic.

"Where're you going?"

"I'm going to tell Clint what I think of him," she replied, her teeth clenching before my eyes.

"You're not doing anything," I said.

Elena's gaze went from my face to Ginessa's, and then back again. Denise just sat in silence.

"He just embarrassed you in front of a bunch of people, and your response is to do nothing?"

By now, the meal was sticking like glue where it had landed. I could feel the ingredients hardening all over me.

"Yes," I said adamantly. "Sit down, please."

We had a brief stare down, and for the first time in my life, I didn't look away. Maybe fear really did change your life. It did at this moment.

After a stretch of awkward silence, Ginessa conceded.

"Fine," she said, and then sat down and unzipped her book bag. She pulled out three Spam sandwiches and handed one each to her friends. She slid hers out of its Ziploc bag. The bread was toasted, and when she took a bite, scrambled eggs fell onto the plastic. Fried Spam was in the center of it.

I inhaled. It smelled just like a Sunday morning at my house, one of the go-to breakfasts that Mom used to make. It smelled like security and comfort, despite the chaos around us. Sunday was the only day all of us were together. And it was one of the only times I didn't mind being a part of the family. Food really did bring people together.

Without looking at me, she said, "There's one in there for you. In case you're hungry." She chewed a bite. "There's also some paper towels and a bottle of water."

When the laughter had died down around us, she snuck a look at Clint and his crew, who at this time were mimicking me by holding spaghetti up to their faces and hair.

My eyes dashed around the schoolgrounds, observing the rest of the student body in attendance, the heavy stares falling upon me. Pulling out the paper towels and wetting them with the water, I wiped off the mess of food from my face and hair.

Reaching for the extra Spam-wich, I said, "I didn't know you made sandwiches."

Ginessa nodded.

"I wanted to share with them," she said, gesturing to her friends with her head.

I slid the sandwich out from its bag and took a bite. My eyes closed, and for a moment, I was back in our kitchen, sitting around the table, with Mom preparing breakfast, the aroma of salty meat filtering in the air. A smile formed as I remembered how Dad would offer to help cook, but since our kitchen was so small, Mom would force him to sit and spend time with us. In all certainty, Mom just loved taking care of us. Opening my eyes, the reality was more jarring than ever.

I couldn't wait for school to be over.

AND HE'S YOUR RELATIVE?

In my afternoon classes, I experienced minor humiliation from a couple kids who pointed at the visible stain on my shirt. But somehow, I made it to the final class of the day. As I entered the classroom, my guts twisted like a pretzel, and I was sweating baluts!

Here we go again, I thought, knowing my bullies would be in this class.

Miss Francis was writing on the whiteboard as I entered the classroom. She turned her head to greet me when I passed with a quick nod followed by a brief smile. She did a double take at the state of me, then her eyes narrowed and her nostrils twitched.

"Is that spaghetti sauce I smell?" she asked.

The stench was slight, and my hair was somewhat sticky from the spaghetti. I thought I'd ridden myself of any evidence, but I clearly hadn't.

"Yeah," I said. "My lunch got away from me."

Slight laughter from Clint filtered in my direction. The tension immediately rose up my spine. I internally shuddered and kept any accusations to myself. But my eyes drifted over to where he was sitting, and I could tell that Miss Francis was putting two and two together.

"Do you have a shirt you can change into?" she asked. "Like a gym shirt or something?" After more laughter started up, she whipped her head toward the football players, who stopped laughing instantly.

I followed her gaze and found Clint staring at me with a tight smirk until I answered Miss Francis. I didn't want to give him and Bart the satisfaction of, once again, getting to me, so I declined her invitation.

The rest of the kids chatted amongst themselves with an occasional glance to the front where I was frozen in place. I finally snapped out of my stupor and walked to my seat. Only a few of my classmates kept their gaze on me as I sat down.

I felt like I wanted to vomit, my mouth starting to water, so I swallowed as hard as I could. I was completely on edge, anxiety pouring through me like a running faucet. Tightening my jaw, I inhaled deeply and sat still, staring toward Miss Francis.

"Okay, everyone," she began. "Today, I'm giving you time to work on your research papers." She spun on her toes light as a feather, addressing the class in a soft tone. "But before I let you all loose, does anyone have ideas to share?"

I slunk down in my seat, attempting to avoid being seen.

Clint rose from his seat. The desk's legs screeched across the floor as he shoved it away from him, like he was pushing away a tank that had barricaded him against the wall.

"I'll share," he said in a loud, energetic voice.

"Thank you, Clint," Miss Francis said. "The floor is yours." Then she walked over to her desk, her back toward the class.

Clint, taking any opportunity to mess with those beneath him, smacked the back of my head as he paraded to the front.

Ow!

Then he passed by another kid, Jose, brushing the top of the boy's scalp with his palm.

"Hey," said Jose as he ducked and then quickly combed his hair with his hand.

Miss Francis took her seat and looked up toward Clint and I watched as she eyed him for an explanation, but he shrugged like he had no idea what was happening.

Before anything could result from it, Bart and the other jocks clapped, a roar of a sound, encouraging an impromptu applause from the other kids. One by one by one, the rest of the class joined in. And just like that, Miss Francis's attention had dropped and returned to the class.

Mr. Popularity took his position. He addressed the classroom with what some girls called his dreamy eyes and stud-like attitude, smiling with perfectly straight teeth. I could have sworn there were soft swoons filtering throughout the room from a few of the kids sitting near me.

He had it all! Everyone in the school knew that Clint's parents owned a car dealership, one of the largest in the area. He couldn't wait to drop it in a sentence. The star football player, hunky and talented, all the traits that made him who he was: the most popular guy in school.

The dealership commercials played constantly on cable TV and every so often—usually around the holidays or giant sales extravaganzas—the entire family would be displayed prominently in the advertisements. Clint was often the focal point during these ads, standing in his football jersey with a football in one hand, faking a play for the camera and its audience. Computer generated cheers would play underneath and a voiceover would scream, "It's *your* turn to *catch* big savings!" Then Clint would throw the football into the camera.

My bitterness was getting away from me, almost as if it had a mind of its own.

"As you all know," began Clint with a slight, yet confident, smile. He paused with enough silence to gain the attention of every ear within a fifty-mile radius. "My family owns one of the most well-known car dealerships in the area. We're local celebrities, if you ask me."

Oh, please . . .

He glanced around the room and returned to his speech. "But what some of you may not know is that my grandfather, who opened the dealership fifty years ago, was the Hall of Fame quarterback, Sid Luckman. He played for the Chicago Bears and led the team to *four* NFL Championships."

A girl sitting in the front row, impressed by Clint, leaned forward, her elbows propping up her head. Her eyes fluttered whenever he looked in her direction, and she flashed a smile so wide that astronauts could spot it from the International Space Station. Any moment Miss Francis would be wheeling her out on a gurney.

"Tell us more," the girl said swooning.

"Gimme a break," I muttered. A harsh shush came from behind and I flinched. *Did I say that out loud?*

"My grandfather was inducted into the Hall of Fame in 1965," said Clint, thrusting his jaw forward with each word. "He threw for nearly fifteen thousand yards in his career."

A collective "ooh" rang through the room, all in perfect harmony, as if Pentatonix suddenly attended our school. I rolled my eyes.

"My paper will discuss my grandfather's transition from football player to business tycoon," Clint finished. By now, his arrogance was brimming over. With each word, his smile grew wider and his head nodded more fluidly.

A contented sigh came from the front row, and I nearly puked.

Clint's teeth were ghostly white, as if they were bleached two seconds before class. Like he had a team of makeup artists waiting in the wings to freshen him up in between classes and bullying those beneath him.

"Thank you," he said, nodding with assurance.

Applause erupted, led by Bart and the other football players, and before Clint returned to his seat, he said, "And now, I'd like to bring up Bart, whose family has a *sweet* history." He motioned for Bart to come forward.

Bart rushed to the front of the room, bumping into my shoulder—ugh!—when he passed.

"Sorry, bruh," he said to me.

He bro-hugged Clint, who then retreated to his seat. Bart greeted the class and swiftly launched into his family's legacy—a multi-generation-owned confectionery company. For the next several minutes, Bart entertained the classroom with a vague story about his mother inheriting a chocolate company from her grandfather, who'd inherited it from his grandfather, and so on and so on, until he couldn't recall the rest of the timeline and ended his long ramble with, "And I'll bring in some samples for everyone."

Kids in the front row cheered at the last part. Honestly, Bart could have just said that last line and the result would have been the same.

My lips constrained firmly in a straight line, and I crossed my arms. I assumed each football player would present a topic. I was fine with that. Even though my topic was super awesome, it wasn't technically my family heritage. I still wasn't sure if it was a good idea to write about it considering my recent conversation with Lola.

And I was right. Each football player did. Next up was Alexander. He smiled nervously before going into an awkward spiel about his topic, which was either about his mother being a triplet, or his mother having two other siblings that were really close in age.

Miss Francis thanked him. She looked around the room for other volunteers.

"I'll go," Ryan volunteered.

"Go, Ryan!" cheered Clint.

Clapping ensued and the fourth football player marched to the front.

"I'm actually going to talk about my father's time in the short lived, but sorta famous rock band, The Seaside," Ryan said. He gave a brief history of the band and let us know his father sang lead vocals and played harmonica. Then he took his seat.

Clint clapped loudly, which led to more clapping. Before Miss Francis could ask for another volunteer, I heard Bart's voice behind me, "I thought I saw Victor's hand up."

What?

I turned my upper body to face him.

"I thought you were raising your hand," he said, and then he smirked.

Miss Francis, drawing my attention back to the front, said, "Victor?"

My eyes bulged.

"Uh . . ." I started, not knowing what to do.

What could I possibly say that could overshadow how great Clint and Bart's families were?

My parents had nothing on them. Any of them! Two Filipino parents with simple jobs— simple lives. There was nothing super about them. Period. Then, I remembered.

Filipino.
Super.
Superhero.

It was as if the call came from a higher power. Some unknown force that I had no control over. An origin story in the making when the main character was at his lowest. Brought here by a combination of things. In this case, two bullies and a best project title on the line.

"Sure, uh . . . did I ever mention that I—" I cleared my throat. "Have a relative who's a superhero?"

One classmate coughed out a laugh. The news was that abrupt. Inside, I was screaming at myself. *What're you doing?*

"A superhero?" asked Miss Francis cautiously. "You mean, a relative like a police officer or something?"

"Um no, he's a real-life superhero," I answered, my teeth clenched. "He sorta fights crime."

Miss Francis wasn't certain what to think and I should have just stopped right there but the energy surrounding me was too strong. I had no control of my body, almost as if I was bit by a radioactive spider and the venom was taking me over.

"And he's your relative?"

"Yeah."

"And he's a superhero?"

"Yeah. But not with superpowers. More like super abilities."

"And superheroes exist?"

"Yeah. But like I said, he's not like Superman. He's more like Batman. Human, but . . ." She was quiet. "Y-you'll see."

She gestured with her hand to approach the front of the room. I jumped from the seat and hustled. I breathed in deeply to calm my nerves and then spun around to the class to deliver my topic. But before I did, Miss Francis leaned toward me.

"Everything okay?" she whispered.

"Yeah."

"Okay," she said, and then she gave me some room. She seemed concerned, almost like it was the most ridiculous thing she'd ever heard. Maybe it was, but she hadn't seen the video yet.

The video!

The video was what would erase all the humiliation. In my head, a drumroll sounded. Then an introduction: Sensei Tsinelas, Tsinelas, Tsinelas.

The introduction sounded so much grander in my mind, complete with a full band, and I felt hopeful that this would work in my favor.

"His name is Sensei Tsinelas," I said. It was a term I'd coined because it sounded badass.

One girl wrinkled her nose.

Dennis's head cocked slightly.

Cyrus yawned in boredom and disinterest.

Another boy grimaced.

Kelsey, in the back, rubbed her chin.

A boy in front blinked repeatedly.

And Clint just laughed to himself. "Loser," he muttered.

This wasn't what I'd expected. In my mind, I'd hoped for them all to cheer, rush me, and then pick me up like a coach winning the big game. *What have I done?*

Miss Francis sidled up next to me.

"It might help to know what tsinelas means," she said.

"Oh! Tsinelas means slippers in Filipino."

No one said a thing.

I froze and my heart began to race. Then I said, "I have a video I can show."

I pulled out my phone, loaded up the video, and pressed play. At once, the first several rows of teens leaned forward in their seats, like synchronized swimmers competing for a gold medal. Again, in my head this seemed amazing but realizing that my phone was only about five inches in length and the quality of the video was slightly amateurish, I totally got it.

Sadly, it wasn't going as planned.

Miss Francis turned to me. "Can I see the video?"

Then, addressing the class, she said, "Give us just a few minutes."

Five to be exact, I thought.

She pulled me off to the corner of the room.

"I don't want to indulge you with this," she said. "I think you're using this as a coping mechanism because of what happened. I'm pretty certain superheroes don't exist."

"Maybe not superhero, superhero," I said. "You'll see what I mean."

She hesitantly nodded and I restarted the video. It played on and every so often she turned to me and then continued watching. As it got to the slipper throw, her eyebrows shot up.

"I think I remember hearing about this," she said. "It was actually a big deal here."

So she knew.

She glanced into the room. All eyes were on her, waiting in anticipation.

"Why don't we do this," said Miss Francis. "Let's write the link on the board, and we can all watch it on our phones together. But first, some context. This was a semi-big story years ago here in Portland. It was before my time, so I'll just leave it at that."

Miss Francis was always coming up with great ideas. She walked over to me and copied the link for the class to watch along. As she wrote the website URL on the board, I continued rambling, hoping something would resonate with my classmates.

"He uses objects like slippers to fight crime." My voice came out screechy so I cleared my throat. "Like Batman and his utility belt."

"Batman doesn't wear slippers," quipped Alexander.

Miss Francis cut him a look.

The classmates pulled up the video on their respective phones, watching it from beginning to end. There was nothing I could do but stand back and watch. Hope for the best.

A few kids chuckled, then more, and the laughter started to get to me.

"This is super shaky," said one boy.

"What is this?" Ryan asked. "Is this a movie?"

Movie?

"Why can't you see any faces?" said Madelyn.

"If you ask me," Clint said, "it looks fake."

Fake?

"Yeah," Bart added. "You can fake anything and post it online."

Other kids joined in on the bandwagon.

"One time, a friend of mine's brother Photoshopped Harry Styles on the moon landing," howled one girl.

"I think I saw that," Clint said, even though he probably hadn't.

By now, the class was erupting with stories and laughter. Like this was some sort of joke.

"Everyone," said Miss Francis. "Let's settle down and give Victor his time."

The classroom silenced. Slowly, but enough for me to continue.

"Uh, he also does good deeds around the city," I said, remembering our time cleaning up Waterfront Park. "But, as you can see from this video, his main weapon is throwing the slipper."

Kicking off one shoe, I demonstrated a fake throw into the classroom, only to watch the invisible shoe fly across the room and back into my hand like a boomerang. In my head, an imaginary dotted line tailed the invisible shoe.

I waited for some sort of positive response, something to convince me that I was doing the right thing, but I got nothing. Instead, everyone just stared at me like I was some alien. Like Jor-El explaining to Kal-El why he was so different, raised as a human and the only survivor of Krypton, but still not from earth.

Then, Clint said, "Unbelievable." Shaking his head, he continued, "Now you're legit making up stories? All for a presentation?"

One kid laughed and another buried her face in her hands. Instantly, my head turned to Miss Francis. *This is a real thing.* But I didn't say anything. It looked like my plan was a huge failure, and for what, being voted the best project?

Suddenly, one, now two, wait, make that three kids, said that it *could* be real.

"Just because it happened before our time doesn't make it fake," Dennis said. "I mean if anything like this could happen, it could happen in Portland."

"I know," Kelsey said. "There's a unicyclist bagpiper in a Star Wars mask for Christ's sake!"

Cyrus then said, "And if ghosts and aliens exist, why not superheroes?"

Exactly! Why not superheroes?

THIS ONLY WINDOW I NEED

Why not superheroes?

That was all I'd thought about as I approached the food cart for my shift that evening. When I arrived at work, Sir was tending to customers. After bagging up the boxes for an order, he totaled up the amount on his small notepad.

"Twenty-seven dollars," he said. "I threw in extra sauce for the lumpia." He smiled. "Enjoy!"

The patrons retrieved their meals and walked away. I entered the cart and inhaled the smell of freshly cooked food mixed with frying peanut oil. I loved this smell and although I'd normally felt at ease, I could barely contain my enthusiasm.

"Kumusta," Sir said when he saw me. "Have you eaten?"

How could I eat at a time like this? I'd just got some validation from a few classmates about my superhero theory. And now here I was. In the presence of greatness. My heart pounding in excitement, I waved him off, and instead took my position at the window next to him. He slid over to make room, the two of us with our elbows propped on the window's ledge, staring out into the city.

"Has it been busy?" I asked.

"Good flow. Seems to be slowing down," said Sir. "Nothing I can't handle."

"Even if it was super busy, you'd still be able to get orders out, juggle some Mahjong tiles, and save the world."

He giggled.

"I don't know about save the world," he said. "But I make sure people fed."

I smiled because everything he said supported my theory. Downtown looked peaceful from my view, the eastside's skyline shadowed as the sun began to settle in the west. I chalked up the city's safeness to Sir ignoring the police's plea to leave the crime solving to them. In reality, he was fighting crime under everybody's noses. Including mine. Just then, a customer approached the window.

"Good evening," Sir greeted. "How may we help?"

"I called in an order," the man said.

Sir retrieved a plastic bag tied at the top filled with several to-go boxes.

"Aiden?"

"That's me."

"Enjoy." He passed the bag to Aiden, who inhaled the aroma and disappeared down the street.

"How was school?" Sir asked. "Learn anything good?"

Here was my opening!

"It was fine," I said, shrugging. "Although I do have to write something on the Great Recession. I was thinking I would talk about the Occupy Wall Street movement and how it resulted in protests across the country."

"Great Recession?" he asked. "Sound complicated."

"It shouldn't be too bad," I responded. "I've been doing some research. If there was anything my parents taught me, it was, to be a good student, you had to do some research."

Most of this was the truth at least.

"Research important," said Sir. "Always lead you to where you want to go."

"I agree. Like I read that there was a huge demonstration in Pioneer Square," I said. "But I was too young for that." Clearing my throat, I asked, "What about you? You were here in Portland, right?"

"Yeah, I here."

"Did you participate in any of the Occupy Portland events?"

My eyes drifted toward Sir, seeing if anything sparked the question. He was coy as coy could be.

"Not sure what you mean."

"Back like ten years ago," I said. "Maybe twelve. There was a huge protest in the square. Something like ten thousand people attended. If you were here, I'm sure you would've heard about it."

"Doesn't sound familiar," he said. "But if true, could be why I was so busy that day."

"So, you remember?"

"No," he said, chuckling to himself. "Always busy it seems."

I felt like he was trying to distract me from learning his secret. I asked again. "You don't remember the Occupy Portland event? I heard there was commotion that made the news."

Sir started fidgeting and I could sense he was uncomfortable. A vast difference from his typical jovial demeanor just a few moments ago.

"Wait," I motioned with my finger. Pulling out my phone from my pocket, I pulled up the video. "I think there was footage of it."

By now, the video had gained more than a million views. Sir's eyes bulged as he watched. It was like he saw a ghost. He stared at the video without ever making eye contact with me.

"Where this come from?"

"The internet," I said. He displayed a look of pure confusion. "Don't you surf the web?"

"No time," he said. "I hate all the windows." Then he gestured to the cart's rectangular opening. "This only window I need. Window to customers."

The clip played on, and for the next five minutes, Sir watched in both horror and concern. The video ended, and he slowly pushed the phone away from himself in disgust.

"Ay," he muttered. "Susmaryosep."

These were the exact words he uttered when I'd witnessed the tsinelas throw.

"This *is* you in the video!" I nearly screamed in happiness. "Isn't it?"

Instead of admitting that he was the vigilante, he said, "Why you ask?"

"I was, um, wanting to write about you and your heroics," I pushed out. "And maybe you could come to my class for the presentation." Stammering, I said, "Another kid is bringing chocolates for everyone. Could be cool."

"This for Great Recession topic?"

I'd completely made up that topic to broach the subject so I could see why he was so confused. I decided to come clean.

"Not exactly," I said. "But it is for a paper and presentation."

"What you mean, Victor?" There was sternness in his voice, almost as if he was losing his temper with me. Which was unusual; I'd never seen him act this way.

"Well . . . like a show-and-tell. To talk about the slipper throw," I said. "I want to do my paper and presentation about you."

My gaze then landed on Sir, who was now staring at me under half-lidded eyes.

"So, if not for Great Recession, what is it for?"

Here it was. My chance to propel myself from tool to cool kid. To add the *eee* to Victor and make it victory. To give my life's theme song an upbeat tempo.

I started from the beginning—the family tree project, how poorly it went, Clint and his bullying (and not just me, but all the nerdy kids in school), and now the research paper.

"And when I saw you foil that robbery with your slipper and now this video," I said. "It dawned on me. That's what I need to write about."

Sir's forehead creased and his eyes strained. His finger scratched at his chin. I really wasn't sure what he was thinking at this moment.

"So, will you come to my school?" I swallowed the built-up saliva in my mouth. "After all, I remember when me and my sister came here, you joked about her teaching me about my culture."

Sir didn't answer straight away. Instead, his head fell backward, his eyes staring up toward the sky. His hips swayed from side to side, almost like he was in a daze.

He was thinking about something.

The inside corners of Sir's brows slanted upward. His cheeks then raised, and a string of muffled words left his mouth.

What was he saying?

"I sorry to hear about your bully," he said. "But I don't think that good idea."

Before I could utter a sound, much less say a word, a couple approached the window, squashing any momentum that was building. Sir acknowledged the two with a smile.

Turning to me, he said, "Take orders. We have work to do."

"But!"

Sir told the couple I'd help, and then he walked back to the kitchen. I rang up the order, told them it would be a few minutes, and then sulked in the corner.

After we filled the order, Sir said that it was time to close. The hours were posted on the cart, but most of the time we didn't follow them. He usually determined when to close based on foot traffic and how much food there was in the cart. Following his instructions, I pulled out the garbage bag and knotted the plastic drawstrings.

"Taking the trash out," I said.

Sir nodded and cleaned up the kitchen, wiping down the counters and placing each item back in its place.

When I stepped out of the truck, the lot seemed empty. Hardly any customers were around, and the other food carts were following suit by closing up for the day. Filipino Feast looked dark even though there were overheard streetlamps illuminating the area. It was almost as if the food carts were already closed.

I walked to the community dumpster and lifted the lid to heave the trash bag into it. The door on the food truck closed behind me, and Sir stepped off the cart and onto the cement. Just then, someone came up behind him and jammed something in his back. I couldn't tell what it was from my point of view, but I could tell it was a robbery. I slinked behind the dumpster in fear.

"Gimme what's in the register," the robber said. His black mask was pulled tight over him, giving me only a shape of his head. I could see the shape of his eyes but nothing really substantial jumped out at me under this low of lighting. "Now!" he screamed.

Sir's eyes then narrowed, and in one quick motion, he spun around, grabbed the robber's arm, twisted it down in front him so fast that the robber did a somersault, landing on his back. Sir bent down and pulled off his slipper and raised it above his head. The robber screamed in pain, quickly stood up, and ran off.

Sir just stood there. He looked badass if I could ever describe someone.

"That was incredible," I said, emerging from my hiding place. My presence must have jarred him because instantly Sir played it off by dropping the tsinelas on the ground and sliding his foot into it.

"Not incredible," he argued. "Just got lucky."

"What do you mean luck—"

"Let's go," he cut me off. "Time to go home."

VICTOR DELA CRUZ DAY

Popularity came at a price, and for this paper and presentation to be great, I wasn't sure how much I'd have to pay. I already broached the topic, and since a few kids in class were on my side, there was no other option than to present the Legend of Sensei Tsinelas with a bang! Even though Lola and Ginessa would never approve of this. And especially since Sir declined to come even after what I'd witnessed.

At this point, how would he even know?

Stacks of sticky notes that I'd jotted on for reference surrounded my desk. The desk looked like one of those FBI manhunts, with sticky notes and pieces of yarn tacked together like a flowchart that led to photographs of potential crime bosses. Okay, so it was only three Post-its with a pic of Sir in the middle. All pointing to the main subject—Sensei Tsinelas, the name I'd given Sir. My eyes dashed around the notes, as if I was decoding some sort of secret message that would ultimately save my life, and I plugged away on the keyboard with great ambition.

Lola quietly entered my room. Her sudden appearance surprised me. I finished writing a sentence and then stopped, the side of my mouth twisting from the unwanted distraction. She wasn't excited about my idea when I'd first brought it up, but it was too late now, and I only hoped she would understand the importance.

"Hey," I said, my back to Lola, my fingertips firm on the keyboard, itching to type the next words.

"Wanted to see how the paper is coming along." Her eyes peered around me, and she bit her bottom lip in curiosity. "I mean, after our initial discussion. Did you need any help?"

"I don't think so," I said. "It's going well."

I was short in my reply, my eyes burning into the screen, and the apparent stiffness in my chest was a dead giveaway. Deep down, it wasn't going well. The paper was mostly made up, and as cool as it sounded in my head, when I talked about it in class, I knew that I'd opened a whole new world.

But what could have I done?

I already was one of the biggest nerds in school who wore superhero shirts every day, so winning best presentation would make high school totally worth it. Nearly four years of being a nobody would be erased. Just like that. And what about those who were onboard with this? I wasn't just doing this for me, I was doing this for all the nerds and unpopular kids.

"It doesn't seem like you're doing well," she prodded. She moved to the corner of the bed and sat on the duvet. I slid my chair away from her, closer to the desk. She sighed. "Now, what's going on?"

Gazing doubtfully into the warm glow of the computer screen, I frowned, the words on the screen jumbling together into a series of nothingness. I had to make this paper good . . . make that great, but all I could think about was Clint saying how I faked the video.

Sighing, I spun around on the seat and addressed Lola, my face pallid. She leaned back to give me space and after a deep breath, I decided to come clean.

"It's just . . . I need this paper to be great."

"Oh?" She paused. I could tell she was thinking about what to say but she said nothing.

"The class is voting on the best project. It would be so cool to win," I said. "Plus, if I can nail this assignment, I'll become someone worth hanging out with. Someone memorable. And not just for being me."

Lola nodded.

"And this is important to you?" she asked. "You're already special, and it just seems like you're trying too hard to force this assignment."

"I don't think you understand what I'm going through," I said.

"So, tell me."

I thought about all the bullying and name calling but I couldn't drum up the courage to tell her. It was just too much for me.

"You can tell me anything," she said.

"Before, you criticized me for not getting involved with my heritage," I said. "Now that I am, you're saying I'm trying too hard." I shrugged. "I just don't get it."

Lola sat back.

"I want you to learn about where you and your family came from," she explained. "Get to know your history, and you can do that by writing about your family." Pursing her lips, she shook her head. "Now you're trying to write about something that isn't you. About a made-up superhero."

He's real, I thought.

"Is there something else going on here?" she asked.

My chin lowered and a buildup of tears started to form behind my eyes. It was time to open up.

"It's important to me because I'm not popular. I look at my brown skin and I'm ashamed. Then I see how others look at me—this nerd who's into superheroes."

"I see," said Lola. She touched her lips with her fingertip, her gaze falling to the floor as her body stiffened. After a second, she returned her attention to me. "Do you think it's going to work?" Her eyes brushed across my notes. "Your paper? Is your paper going to make you popular? Do you think it'll win best presentation?"

Maybe, I thought.

"I showed the video," I said. My body sank and I replayed the incident in my head. "But some people said I faked it." Shrugging, I added, "Like I would even know how to do that."

"Couldn't you?"

"Couldn't I what?"

"Fake it. You keep telling yourself that you're a nerd," said Lola. "Maybe they think you're smart enough to manipulate it."

I never considered that.

"I guess," I replied. And then I put my head down.

"So," she said, capturing my attention once again. "You showed the video. What did you want to result from that?" Lola's brows raised and curved across her forehead. She was waiting for a response.

"I don't know. I didn't have time to think about it," I said. "I was put on the spot and the topic came out."

"It seems like you wanted to write about this all along," said Lola. She gestured to the screen and reminded me about our initial conversation. "And it still seems like your plan." I turned to look at the research and then I thought about my conversation with Sir. "So, when you brought it up in class, what were you hoping for?"

It wasn't something that I'd thought through. And perhaps it was something I'd wanted all along, so I guess Clint and Bart did me a favor. And frankly, after I'd brought it up, I didn't consider any reaction short of a town banquet or day reserved in my name for introducing such a treasured commodity.

Victor Dela Cruz Day. Observed.

This would include a parade with various youth groups and a super tall dude walking on stilts. I would think the mayor would show, but who knew what his schedule was like.

But then again, maybe not. After all, he did warn Sir to leave the crime handling to the police. Before I could get lost even more, like to the lumpia eating contest, I saw Lola's eyes burning through me.

"Victor?"

"I guess I didn't think about what could have happened."

"Perhaps not. But let's say that you present your paper," Lola began, "and the other kids love it. In fact, your presentation is voted the best."

She paused and I motioned with my hand for Lola to continue, rotating it over and over. *And? And!* I mentally encouraged her to continue. The lumpia eating contest?

"And then they all love you for *not* who you really are, but for being this giant phony." She pressed her lips into a thin line. "Don't you think that people will like you more for being authentic? What if they find out how big a liar you are? What will you do then?"

Thinking on my feet, my gaze darted around the room, until my eyes fell upon the notes. An idea flashed in my head.

"I know," I said. My eyes beamed, a lightbulb flicking on inside. This was a job for . . . "I can ask Sensei Tsinelas for help." Lola's shoulders dropped, her body sinking into itself. "I know, I know. I'm just kidding."

Dismissing my comment with a quick smirk, she said, "I know your parents were not as exciting as you think but they loved you, and I think you're doing a disservice by not writing about them. They might surprise you. And considering what happened, you owe it to them to honor them." Her eyebrows raised. "Maybe talk about them and also about being a Filipino teenager in the United States?"

I was born and raised in the States. *Look at me*, I thought. Being Filipino in the U.S. wasn't interesting. No one wanted to hear about a brown-skinned white kid growing up in a Filipino family who knew nothing about being Filipino and solely adopted white culture in an effort to blend in. I opted to pass.

"But I have to make it awesome!" I said. "I have to win."

I reminded myself about how amazing the legend of Sensei Tsinelas was. I wouldn't get that same feeling if I presented my own history, and I really didn't want to let that go. I mean, nobody was impressed by me in person. I couldn't imagine anyone being impressed by me on paper. As if I would somehow *wow* them with a PowerPoint.

The Lameness of Victor Dela Cruz. A presentation.

Slide one, meet Victor.

Slide two, laugh and tease uncontrollably.

And slide three, watch me do nothing.

"I already brought it up," I said. "And I'm already knee-deep in research and it's halfway written," gesturing to the notes and my laptop, "So I think my best plan is to continue forward."

The excuses slipping off my tongue were a waterfall of empty words. I wasn't about to give Clint and Bart the satisfaction. If I changed course now, I couldn't imagine how they would treat me afterward.

Lola smiled half-heartedly.

"Well, he must really be something special then," she said. "I hope this works out for you."

Stealing a glance at the screen, in the center of the scattered notes, I nodded. The cursor was blinking on the page.

"Thanks," I muttered.

How could I convince her that what I was doing was right? How could I—I know!

I clicked on a tab that was open for reference. The window pointed to an article in the *Oregonian*. Positioning the laptop so Lola could see, I gestured with a quick turn of my head.

"Read this really quick." I situated the computer in front of her eyes. Lola squinted so she could read the small, pixelated content.

Portland vigilante foils would be robbery

Published: Apr. 25, 2010, 8:20 p.m.

By Jamie McFade | *Oregonian*

Christmas is usually a time for joy. But it is also a time of stress, especially when you're working on a budget. Most people working with a limited pocketbook result to more creative ideas such as making their gifts or offering grand gestures. One Portland resident, feeling the holiday squeeze, chose a different route.

As nervous shoppers scrambled to find gifts for their loved ones, one shopper, 25-year-old Lawrence Carrole, scrambled out the door with a newly released hardcover book from Powell's City of Books in downtown Portland.

Carrole slid the book into an inner pocket of his coat and nonchalantly walked toward the exit. The book's stock was low, and the bookstore was not anticipating another shipment until after the new year, according to a Powell's employee who wished to stay anonymous.

In a Christmas miracle, a clerk stocking shelves witnessed the entire event. As Carrole made his way to the open area just inside the store's entryway, the clerk alerted those in attendance with a high-pitched scream. An onlooker compared her voice to a whale.

"It was the loudest thing I'd ever heard," the onlooker told the *Oregonian*.

The scream caused Carrole to sprint toward the front exit. In another miracle, a vigilante saw the commotion through the bookstore's large glass windows. It was so chaotic that he managed to blend into the crowd with ease.

According to another eyewitness, the scene was described as follows: a young man was bolting to the exit, a female clerk was pointing and screaming, and spectators nearby were observing the scene in panic.

"I just remember watching him leave the store and looking around," the eyewitness said. "The intersection was crazy and there was a street performer playing his guitar and singing 'Jingle Bells.'"

That's when the eyewitness said that Carrole made a mistake. "He hesitated too long," the eyewitness said.

It all went downhill from there. A vigilante in the right place and right time reached into his inner coat pocket, pulled out what appeared to be nunchucks, and slung it at the shoplifter's feet.

"It was the most amazing thing I've ever seen," the eyewitness said. "It spun in the air like a flying disc, wrapped around the robber's legs, tightened, and then tripped him up."

Lola's mouth grew into a slight grin as she finished the story. At the end of the post was a link to the Occupy Portland video. Her eyes danced in delight.

"He's impressive, that's for sure," she said. "First, one of his tsinelas? And now this?"

"I know," I replied. "I just found this article!"

However, her enthusiasm was short lived.

"I just don't think . . ." she began and then stopped. Nodding curtly, she continued, "Well, you're old enough to make your own decisions."

SECOND COUSIN ONCE REMOVED

I hacked away at my paper until the wee hours of the morning. There were so many ideas that I wanted to capture to make it awesome, so I dove in while they were fresh in my mind.

I'll show everyone, I thought.

Since there was no information on Sir's life, and I'd referred to him as Sensei Tsinelas, I would just have to make it up, building on what I'd already discovered. Nobody would know but me. I'd connect the dots to even the flow of the story, casually dropping tidbits of my life into his to make it our life. Our superhero life, that was. That was really the key—wait and weave myself into parts of the narrative so the story ran together nicely. So it was believable. An origin story for the ages.

Okay . . . Sir owned a food cart. But where did he come from?

I randomly searched the middle of the country, miles away from the Pacific Northwest, and I landed in the heartland, on the border of Illinois and Iowa. Personally, I'd never met anyone from these states, and frankly, they kind of sounded made-up.

Eye-owe-uh? I owe a what? I giggled to myself. It almost looked like the center of America. A place where John Deere tractors were from. And what was more American than that?

I stared at the screen for a few moments, then started typing.

Sir had set up shop in an empty park downtown, just off the Mississippi River. Nearly several brutal months of slow business had passed before winter came. Old man winter with its bitter temper. A winter so brutal Sir was forced to close shop for at least four months, and after his revenue had seen record dips as low as the air temperature, he decided to move to a warmer climate.

Sir read about Portland's food cart initiative in a syndicated article in his hometown newspaper. Based on this random story, he made the trip out west with the little belongings that he had.

He saw Portland's rich history with food carts as an opportunity. The city's loose restrictions and the hippie movement of the '60s had melded to create a unique environment, and not just a means to offer food to residents. Food carts were a lifestyle. This was something Sir could work with—so long as he could find the money for a cart.

I clicked on a random story about a small-time entrepreneur who discovered that old guitars could be repurposed as unique desktop computers. It was simple how he'd come up with the idea. The big hollow body of an old acoustic guitar was butted up against his desktop computer. After a few weeks, he moved the desktop behind the instrument to hide it from view. Then, the idea hit: take the guts of the computer and place them inside the guitar. His invention was born!

The short bio inspired the creativity within, hitting me like I imagine Sir's slipper smacking me would—hard.

It was like my fingers had a mind of their own, the words flowing across my computer screen. Where there were blind spots, I filled them in with my own imagination. Where there were summaries, I expanded. And when specific details were needed, I googled the crap out of them.

Did you know that the very first food cart was credited to the Oscar Mayer Wienermobile?

I paused to reflect on what I was writing. But then Lola's voice crept into my head.

Don't you think that people will like you more for being authentic? What if they find out how big a liar you are? What will you do then?

Should I even be doing this? What if it backfires? What if I end up in the same place as before? Is that even possible? What if it's worse? I mean, they'd basically know I made all of this up.

My hands started to sweat, so much so that my fingers kept sliding off the keys and typing nonsense. I stopped short and deleted the garbage on the screen. Then I slowly sighed, breathing out every negative thought that consumed me.

Once my body felt normal again, as normal as it could be, I pushed forward.

As I invented a good bulk of Sir's history, I started to incorporate myself into the paper, peppering in my family like I would season a bland-tasting soup.

One story involved my family spending a holiday dinner with Sir. Mom and Dad were always generous with their space even if we didn't know the guest intimately. So they invited him over for a nice meal and conversation after they'd met him, shortly after we first discovered Filipino Feast.

At first, Sir refused, saying that the cart would need someone to tend to it.

"But it's Christmas," Mom said. "No one should be alone on Christmas." She perused the rest of the carts and claimed that all the other businesses would be closed as well. Dad even confirmed with the Italian cart a few spaces down.

This was something my parents had always done. I was just tweaking reality now. Honestly, the real event was based on one of my uncles on Dad's side who was traveling up from California to Canada during the holiday season.

But wait. An important missing factor popped into my head. How was he related to me? My eyes rolled across the ceiling. An uncle? A cousin? What about a second cousin once removed? I bit down on my bottom lip. I had to make this not only believable, but like Superman—bulletproof. If Sir was my second cousin once removed, it would make him my great-granduncle's grandchild. Right? And saying that he was my second cousin once removed wouldn't draw suspicions because really, what was that? Being a second cousin once removed was like being from Iowa. Nobody would question that!

I remembered the family tree project, tracing the branches for any cousins I could associate Sir to. And there it was. A lone name that sounded so perfect for a superhero's identity: Benito Arguello. He was the Hal Jordan of Filipino superheroes. Sir was my second cousin once removed.

Secret identity: Benito Arguello
Superhero name: Sensei Tsinelas
Profession: Food cart owner/chef
Superpowers: None
Abilities: Tsinelas Throw, microphone nunchucks, food magic

BOOM!

The Christmas holiday that Sir had shared with my family was one of the best that I could remember. The dishes were traditional in the American sense that there was ham and turkey, with all the sides like stuffing, mashed potatoes, and green bean casserole.

But with my Filipino background, the dinner also included staples that I had grown up with: white rice, pancit, chicken adobo, and lumpia rolled and compressed into tiny cigars so tight you could hand them out to newborn fathers.

Mom and Dad cooked all the food. They'd wanted Sir to have a day off—even if it was just one—and had insisted that he make himself at home. That wasn't by accident. Filipinos offer their homes to anyone. You could be on the lam and Filipinos would offer you food, a bed, and the title of "uncle". That was until you were indicted, of course.

Sir did, however, offer to bring the lumpia. He picked one up and showed it to me.

"Do you know why I roll these so tightly?" By coincidence, I was about to pop one into my mouth. I stopped and shook my head. "Rolling them this tight keeps the heat in." My eyes moved to the lumpia in my hand. "That way they stay hot for a long time. Long after they been fried." I could feel a slight burn on my fingertips.

I bit into the roll, and straight away, my eyes bulged, the heat now on my tongue.

The juice from the lumpia squirted into my mouth like a bug splattering on the windshield. The burn careened around my mouth, detouring off my tongue, taking the off-ramp to my inner cheek, and then U-turning around my front upper teeth until it bounced up and down off my uppers and lowers like a pinball racking up points to earn a free game. Wherever the juice touched, there was a burning sensation. I had no choice but to chew faster.

"He just told you that they were hot!" Ginessa said, pointing at me and attempting to contain her laughter.

"H-h-hot!" I screamed, chewing the scalding lumpia. With my eyes watering, I slammed the glass of water that was next to me. Those in attendance—Mom, Dad, Lola, Ginessa, and Sir — laughed in unison.

The early morning was creeping through the blinds into my room by now, waking me up from my computer-induced coma. The rising sun in the distance, a reddish glow that filled the landscape, drew my attention to the window. The sun's rays shined new life into me, a turning point. As if this superpower was passing through my body, giving me the strength to go out with a bang.

School was in a couple hours, but I hadn't even inserted myself in any heroics. Nobody wanted to hear about a Christmas dinner where I'd embarrassed myself by eating super-hot lumpia! No matter how on-brand the story was.

C'mon, Victor! Get. It. Together!

I focused on the blinking cursor, pressing my finger to my cheek and propping my chin on the rest of my curled fingers.

Where can I help?
What can I do?
How can I make this amazing?

Closing my eyes, an idea sparked. My eyes shot open, and I got to work with the diligence of Stephen King.

What else could Sensei Tsinelas use to be amazing?
And where could I fit in?

My hand lowered off my face, my finger moving to my chin and scratching it ever so softly. What would go well with a story about a second cousin once removed/Filipino food cart owner/superhero?

I drummed up a story involving a group of terminally ill children.

On an ordinary day like any other, Sir had phoned about his visit to the hospital, asking if I wanted to help with a special surprise that would hopefully brighten the children's day, if only for an hour.

Since Portland wasn't known for snowy weather and many of the kids would not see snowflakes very often, Sir wanted help creating a winter wonderland. He described the snow in the Midwest, how it fell throughout the day and night until it covered the entire city like a heavy blanket. Often, five or six blankets—the thick kind.

The first snow was always the prettiest: the snowflakes sifting down to the ground, creating a thin layer of sparkle. Each flake different from one another in structure but similar in feel, dissolving into a small droplet of water that tickled the skin.

Sir wanted to replicate that for the children, both the scenery and the feeling, as a way to share an experience that he'd cherished back in the Midwest.

Unfolding the top of a ratty, old cardboard box, Sir showed me his stash.

"I have many Capiz shells," said Sir. He eyed a couple other boxes nearby, just as beat-up as the first, all filled with the shells. "Tons."

The insides of the boxes glittered before my eyes, the smoothness of the shells' exteriors shining off the light whenever Sir moved them. They slinked back and forth, shimmying alongside each other with a soft rustling sound.

I ran my fingertips across the smooth, fragile shells, as if grazing a bunch of corn flakes in a box of cereal to find a buried toy. But I didn't find anything. My imagination was running wild with how authentic they felt on my skin.

"I've seen these before," I said, my voice raising in pitch in excitement. "Mom and Dad had a lamp that was made from these."

And then my fantasy life morphed into a memory of my parents. I remembered the Capiz light fixture hanging in the corner of our living room. When the lamp was turned on, the shells created a neat display on the walls around it. Sadly, I never once asked about it. Had I, Mom would have certainly given me a history lesson and probably a neat story as well.

I sniffled, the sudden memory nearly drawing tears to my eyes. Shaking my head, I continued.

"Yes," Sir said. My eyes focused on the intricate grooved ligaments of the off-white shells. "They're really big in the Philippines. People harvest them, turn them into lamps and jewelry."

That was something Mom would say.

"They're beautiful," I said. "And so lightweight." I grabbed a handful of shells and let them fall through my fingertips inside the box.

"Or," explained Sir as he raised the box above my head. "Can use them as snowflakes." Then he flipped the treasure trove over for the shells to trickle out.

The scene was magical—the shells flitting down on top of me, like falling leaves swaying left to right—and I imagined the expressions on the children's faces, similar to the one I was sporting.

Filipino Santa.

"They're going to love this," I said, my smile wide and static.

And they did. Fake or otherwise. Just as I had with my own experience with Capiz shells in real life.

The paper was moving along but now I needed something extraordinary. Something that would really catapult this presentation. After all, I was presenting a superhero. Now it was time to go from mild-mannered Sir to superhero Sensei Tsinelas.

I thought about all the triggers that got me to this point; all of them involved two people. I landed on a story where Sensei and I rescued Ginessa from kidnappers.

Sensei had choreographed some action moves and at this moment, I was doing my best to commit them to memory. *Kick this way! Punch that way! And jump!*

My fingers began to tighten, so I stretched them out while I read the narrative. My gaze instantly found the collage of superheroes spanning across a large part of my bedroom wall. It was a battle scene I'd put together from decals I had purchased over time. The scene took weeks to finish but it was worth it. Nodding, I thought, *Stan Lee would be proud.*

Then, a knock came at the door. Lola.

"You're up already?" she asked.

"Uh, yeah?" I lied, as I hadn't yet slept. "Just working on my paper."

"I see. How is it coming along?" Her voice was soft, gentle. "Care to talk about it?"

Turning to address her, I said, "I don't think so, but you will be happy to know that I have stories in here about Mom and Dad." I pointed to my screen with my chin. Words and words filled it. The length was close to the required page count. "Just got one more part to add, and I should be done for now."

"Well, I'm glad you got a lot accomplished," she said. "And even more glad that your mother and father made an appearance." She looked down the hall. "I guess I'll check on Ginessa." And then she was gone.

I returned to my paper. *Where was I?*

I read and reread the story, adding in my own inadequacies to add realism to the tale. Outside my door, I could hear Ginessa in the bathroom, the shower running. I checked the time; it was almost time to go to school. But in my paper, it was kick-butt/save Ginessa time!

We approached the building where the kidnappers were holding Ginessa. The nerves filtered into my body, my heart beating faster and faster.

"We need a theme song," I mentioned casually. "Something to fight to like in the movies."

"Theme song, like trouble, find you," said Sensei. "Not other way around."

Before we could continue the conversation, the two kidnappers, Clyde and Brad, appeared.

Looking Sensei up and down, Clyde said, "I don't believe you're a superhero." He turned to Brad and goaded him to play along.

Sensei stood in khaki pants with the bottoms rolled up, displaying white socks with tsinelas. He was wearing a formal Filipino shirt called a *barong* over a white sleeveless undershirt. His belly was round and sagged slightly over his belt buckle. I had to give it to Clyde; he didn't look anything like a superhero.

"There's no way you're a superhero," said Brad.

"Superhero," said Clyde, shaking his head. "More like super zero." Then he laughed. Brad joined in and the two laughed diabolically like Dr. Evil in *Austin Powers*. "Look at you! Who could ever be afraid of you?" He chuckled harder.

Brad was holding Ginessa. Abruptly, he pushed her over to our direction.

"You're who we really wanted," Clyde said. "Here's your stupid hostage back!"

I told Ginessa to stand back while Clyde and Brad crouched into fighting positions. Sensei unbuttoned his barong, slid it off, whipped it over to the corner of the building, and then flexed his out-of-shape biceps. His bare arms were dry and for the most part, clear of any visible scars or muscles. But he did have a tattoo that covered his right bicep—a crucifix made from lumpias.

"I love your tattoo," I said.

Bowing, Sensei said, "Thought it was funny, it makes me giggle." Then he flexed and released repeatedly. "Lumpias look like they're dancing." I agreed and laughed along with Sensei.

"Enough!" screamed Clyde.

The loud scream returned my attention to the fight, and my eyes darted to Clyde, who was rushing Sensei.

"Susmaryosep!" said Sensei.

In one quick motion, Sensei pushed me out of the way and whipped out a pair of microphone nunchucks from his pocket. He spun them over his head and then tucked one karaoke microphone under his armpit. With his left hand, he reached into his other pocket and pulled out some barbecue shish kebabs.

When Clyde was close, Sensei snapped the microphone nunchucks and the end struck Clyde's chin, knocking him backward.

BOOM!

"Ow!" Clyde screamed.

Then it was Brad's turn.

Sensei jabbed the shish kebabs at his face. It was so quick that the smell of grilled pork forced Brad to open his mouth, luring him in like a siren's song. Sensei jammed the sticks into Brad's mouth. On instinct, Brad bit down hard onto his tongue. The pain caused him to jump up and down screaming, then stumble over.

Brad hit the ground. Then Clyde, shaking off the former strike, rejoined the fight, coming in on Sensei's blind side.

Crap! I needed to help.

I hustled over to intercept Clyde but instead tripped over myself, inadvertently diving at him and landing short. My fumble caused him to turn his head. And he laughed and pointed.

"Loser," he said.

"No, I'm not," I replied. "You are."

The pathetic comeback was enough for him to turn his full attention toward me. Then he came at me. I wasn't sure what I was going to do at this point, as my fighting skills were non-existent.

I slid back toward the perimeter of the warehouse, with Clyde approaching fast. I felt my body cower, curling into a fetal position like it'd been trained to do since birth. *What should I do? What should I do?* Just as he was about to pounce, I remembered something. The arsenal of weapons we'd gathered for this battle!

I pulled out a balut from my pocket, cracked the shell, and shoved it into Clyde's face.

The mangled duck fetus, its legs all janky and face distorted into something unseen to Clyde, scared the living daylights out of him. Like really, really scared him.

"What the hell is that?" he screamed, his eyes widening like Thanksgiving Day Parade balloons. Any wider and they would've popped out of their sockets.

"It's a duck embryo." I laughed impishly. Clyde fake vomited, his mouth straining open. "It's a delicacy," I said. "And it's delicious!"

"Disgusting!" Clyde shrieked, dismissing the sight with a quick shake of his head. He was so repulsed he stepped backward into the wall, bumping the back of his head.

BOOM!

Brad jumped to his feet, motioning to Clyde, who'd recovered from the balut, and the two charged me.

"Ay!" Sensei called out. I turned. Sensei gestured to his bag.

"What?"

Sensei's lips pursed and extended outward.

"Get lumpia from my bag," he ordered. I did. Peeling back the aluminum foil, the steam escaped into the building, the smoke forming the letters *S* and *V*. I pushed the scalding fried rolls to the kidnappers, who'd stopped short when they smelled the lumpia's aroma.

Clyde and Brad bit into fried rolls and the scorching ingredients squirted into their mouths, burning their insides up and down. Both kidnappers spit out the lumpia and fanned their face.

"H-h-h-h-hot!"

I chuckled.

"Hot, aren't they?"

Once Clyde recovered, he said, "That's it! You're dead meat!" But it didn't sound like that because his mouth was on fire. It sounded more like, "*Thaft fit. Yert deh may!*" Then he and Brad rushed me.

Sensei joined and the epic battle continued, choreographed and all, from how we'd practiced earlier. When Sensei turned one way, I turned the other. When Sensei jumped, I jumped with him. And when Sensei struck his nunchucks, I ducked out of the way.

The nunchucks clocked Clyde and Brad simultaneously.

POW!

Together, we looked like we were dancing a Filipino dance routine. The only thing missing was folk music.

Then we transitioned into the finale. I ran up to Sensei, grabbed hold of his right arm, and then hopped up and sat on his forearm, extending one leg as Sensei spun me around, knocking Clyde and Brad every time they charged us. It was like a bowling ball knocking over the two remaining pins. Over and over.

BOOM!

BOOM!

POW!

Then it hit me.

BOOM! BOOM! POW!

After several attempts at beating Sensei, Clyde and Brad fell to their knees in exhaustion.

BOOM! BOOM! POW!

Sensei stopped spinning, and I slid off his arm and onto my feet. I felt exhilarated, a rush I'd never experienced before.

"Had enough?" Sensei asked, eyeing the two as he settled into form. He kicked off his slipper and whipped it toward Clyde and Brad. The slipper spun in a curve, suddenly curtailing back over the kidnappers' heads. It breezed the tops of their scalps, clipping their skin as a warning strike. They flinched. Sensei raised his hand in the air and the slipper spun directly into his palm. He dropped it to the floor and slid his foot inside as if nothing ever happened. It was magical to say the least!

The lumpia crucifix did a celebratory shimmy on his bicep. Maybe it was twerking, I wasn't certain. Nevertheless, it danced like no one was watching.

"Ready?" Ginessa called into my room, disrupting my groove for a moment. I quickly raised my finger, gesturing for her to hold on.

Clyde screamed, rubbing his eye as it slowly started to swell.

"We give up!" He raised his hand in defeat. Brad followed, one eye a darkish hue, and conceded victory to Sensei. And to me, his sidekick.

And better yet, a theme song was born: "Boom Boom Pow" by the Black Eyed Peas. I whisper-sang, "Boom Boom Pow," to myself, and suddenly, the image of Filipino BEP member, Apl.de.Ap, appeared in front of me. He smirked, raised his closed fist before me, and I fist-bumped the air as his image slowly vanished.

I was under a spell, but it was all worth it. My paper was amazing!

IT'S HIS SUPERHERO NAME

On our way to school Ginessa was relaying how she decided to make a leche flan for the picnic, a popular dessert found in the Philippines and other former Spanish colonies. But she was short vanilla extract and condensed milk, so she had gone to the store. The recipe Ginessa was using was one that Mom had used to make—my mouth watered at the memory of it.

I couldn't imagine Ginessa's flan being as good as Mom's, but she was willing to try. It was unfortunate that Mom didn't get the chance to teach her how to make it, but Lola would be there to help.

The trip to the grocery store itself was hardly eventful, but what happened while she was standing in line to check out was memorable. Just the inflection in Ginessa's voice and her eagerness in the details indicated that the adventure was worth sharing.

Sadly, I was running on virtually no sleep and was not in the mood whatsoever.

"This guy ran full sprint down the aisle toward the entrance," Ginessa said.

She was sitting across from me as the train passed the campus of Portland State University, her backpack on the seat next to her unzipped with the corner of a notebook peeking out.

I drifted in and out of a stupor. My gaze was half on her and half out the window, the lack of sleep and this project creeping in and out of my brain. Now I was wondering if pulling an all-nighter was worth it. What if my presentation wasn't the best?

Maybe I needed more, I thought.

In front of me, Ginessa's lips were moving rapidly but I wasn't sure what she was saying. Her voice continued blending in with the computerized speaker voice that projected instructions every time the train stopped to pick up or drop off passengers.

"He was holding something in his hand," she said with a tinge of anxiousness. "But I couldn't see what." She raised her palms in front of her, giving me a deep shrug. Shaking off the sleeps, I turned to her. "I was fumbling for the correct amount of change." Her voice grew higher with each word, an apparent anticipation swelling the further she got into her story. "An employee was chasing him."

Suddenly, Ginessa's voice fell silent even though her mouth continued to move. The words disappeared and reappeared as if someone had muted her. I fell into la-la land, dreaming that I, too, was at the grocery store . . . make that the Asian grocery store . . . with Sensei as we shopped for various ingredients to restock the cart's inventory. One of those list items being rice.

Beside me, large burlap sacks of rice lay positioned in a pyramid on a wooden pallet. Sensei was holding a fifty-pound bag in one hand, ready to make his decision before moving on to the next ingredient on his shopping list. He scanned the small piece of paper with his eyes, checking off the list as he collected what he needed.

It brought back a memory of Mom. She was always buying rice, the same sized bag. When she returned home, she'd ask me to go out and retrieve it. The fifty pounds were too much for her, and whenever I threw the burlap sack over my shoulder, I pretended I was a superhero carrying a trapped person out from her burning house.

The memory made me smile. So much so, Ginessa noticed.

Pursing her lips, she said, "Why is that funny?"

I shook my head. I'd been daydreaming and completely missed the end of Ginessa's story. I was so consumed with this project that I ignored what she was saying.

"It, um, wasn't funny?" I guessed.

"Then why were you smiling like that?" She stared at me red-faced, her eyes bulging before me. "He got away," she said. "He stole from these hardworking people. And I got pushed into the counter! I almost got hurt!"

"You almost got hurt?"

"Were you even listening?"

"Sorry," I said. "I was up all night working on an assignment." I waited for her to ask a follow-up question, but instead she just stared at me with disappointment in her eyes.

"You know, you really should . . ." Then she stopped. "Never mind."

She unzipped the main pouch of her backpack and pulled out a notebook to read to herself. Just like that.

I watched for a moment, eager that she would finish her statement. *I should what?*

My eyes flicked across the page Ginessa was studying and my eyebrows crumpled. On the page were random notes and bullet points about a variety of subjects. Subjects I didn't think Ginessa took as a freshman.

I gestured with pinched lips, and in an innocent voice, I asked, "What are you doing?"

"Why do you care?" snapped Ginessa, never taking her eyes off her notebook. Instead, she concentrated harder on whatever it was she was working on, leaning in closer to the page.

The air was thick, and I didn't know how to respond. So I said nothing and sighed.

She pulled the pad to her body and slightly covered the contents with her hands. Like she was hiding it from me. Some secret homework assignment I wasn't worthy of seeing. A secret she wanted to hide from the public.

I didn't want to have this tension between us with all that was going on. She had the picnic to think about, and she was still adjusting to high school.

"I meant, if you needed help with homework, I'm here for you," I said. "I get pretty good grades. Plus, I've probably taken those classes already."

Without addressing me, she asked, "What makes you think I need help?"

"I don't know," I said. "Looks like you have a lot of notes there."

The stiffness in her body seemed to disappear and her eyes flitted toward me.

"Well, I don't, but I appreciate you offering," answered Ginessa. "Even though it seems like you're buried in homework as well."

I slow nodded and then sat back into the seat. The train traveled over the pedestrian bridge. I made it a point each day to look at the submarine that was anchored in the river by the museum. It reminded me of a villain's lair, some sort of headquarters that could sink down into the Willamette and spy on the city undetected. Ginessa's voice refocused my attention on the present.

"Have you requested the day of the picnic off yet?"

"No," I replied.

"And why not?"

"I already told you why I didn't want to go," I said. "Plus, I have this assignment I'm working on."

"And what is this assignment about?" she asked, switching gears just like that.

I explained the paper and corresponding presentation, going back to the family tree project. Ginessa hadn't heard about what'd happened, only that Mom had played a big part in filling out the branches. She saw how excited Mom was that night. It was at that moment Ginessa began to learn about our culture. And it was all because I refused to learn about it.

"I have to write about my family," I said.

A smile lit up on Ginessa's face. She was enthusiastic about it.

"You're writing about Mom and Dad?" she asked. "What a great idea!"

"Sure," I said, dismissing her almost immediately. "They're in there, but I'm actually writing about Sensei Tsinelas."

"Who?"

"Sorry. Sir," I explained. "My boss."

Ginessa's lips pointed, her eyes narrowing. She was frustrated for sure, but she always gave me space.

"Okay," she answered.

"I know. It's supposed to be about *my* family heritage," I said. "As in Victor Dela Cruz's family heritage. And don't get me wrong—Mom and Dad, and you, and Lola are in it. But let's be real. No one wants to hear about that." I shrugged. "And since Sir's also Filipino, I figured I'd write about my family heritage, as a *whole*, as in *Filipino* heritage, and not just about me, per se."

"First of all," she said, her pointer finger shooting up into the air. "Why did you call him Sensei Tsinelas? And second, there's no relation, right?"

I smiled at the first part.

"To answer your first question, Sensei Tsinelas is a name I made up for him," I said. "It's his superhero name. And to your second point, no, he's not related. Not by blood. At least I don't think so."

"I know you think *he's* a superhero, but now do you think *you're* one too?" she quipped sardonically. "I guess you can always check the family tree that Mom did for you." Ginessa was having a field day with this. "If you do, see if I'm listed as a superhero too. OMG, I would love to have lasers shoot out my hands."

"Even if he isn't," I ignored, attempting to reel her back into my agenda. "You said yourself that all Filipinos are basically family, right?"

One of Ginessa's eyebrows raised. Again, I checked the severity. Mainly because I was taking the easy way out: placing the burden onto Ginessa's comment about Filipinos being related in case the project didn't turn out, blaming her for my flimsy justification for writing my paper—even though she was trying to prove a point with all the jokes.

Little did she know, though, that he was a superhero . . .

Slowly crossing her arms at chest level, her eyebrow frozen at its current position, Ginessa said, "You hear how ridiculous this sounds?"

"What're you getting at?" I asked, my emotions coming down from their high.

"There are no such thing as superheroes!" Her voice was raised. She was upset. "Screw you for not writing about our family. This is a perfect time to talk about what happened to Mom and Dad."

"I have a lot going on," I replied.

"I know," she said. "So do I. So does Lola. But life goes on and it's been a year. You should really explore your feelings about their death. You can't keep ignoring them or burying them with your superhero obsession. It's almost like you're trying to move on without dealing with our loss. Like it would help you get over it faster, make you feel better—but it won't." She paused, her eyes dancing left to right to think of what to say next. "You're becoming this person I don't like. I want my big brother back."

"I appreciate you looking out for me," I said. "But I know what I'm doing."

Ginessa adjusted herself when the train stopped.

"You may know what you're doing," she said, her voice soft and brittle. "But have you ever asked me how I'm doing? Or Lola? We lost them too."

She shook her head, and when the doors opened, she ran off.

THE FANS HAVE SPOKEN

Ever since Ginessa left me on the train, I'd been thinking about what she had said. She was right. I hadn't talked to her about Mom and Dad. I hadn't talked to Lola either. Come to think of it, I hadn't really spoken to anyone.

It was the last class of the day. A few classes earlier, I texted Ginessa about requesting the day off for the picnic. Then I rushed to the classroom ahead of the other kids. My goal was to tell my side of the story: that the video wasn't faked and that Sensei Tsinelas was the superhero we needed in our lives.

When I entered the room, there were only a handful of other kids sitting by themselves, each swiping through stories on their phone or playing a game or perusing social media—whatever was necessary to distract each person before the class started.

I checked the clock—a few minutes until start time.

One of the kids, Timothy, nodded at me. He was sitting a couple desks away.

"Your paper sounds rad," he said, eyes brightening. "For the record, I don't think the video was faked." Shrugging, he added, "It wasn't really shot well but that doesn't mean it didn't happen."

What a relief.

"The closest thing I have to a superhero relative is a firefighter uncle." Timothy smiled. "You're so lucky."

Timothy was a smaller-than-average looking boy, short with a slight build. He had sandy brown hair with red cheeks and braces. From what I knew about him, he was pretty smart as well. So, he fit the typical profile for jocks and popular kids to poke fun at. Even though we were in the same class, it was the first I'd spoken to him.

"Firefighters are pretty cool," I replied. "They put their lives in danger too."

"But nothing like your relative." Then he smiled. "So cool."

This was the reaction I was hoping for, why I rushed to class in the first place. I wanted to talk about Sensei Tsinelas with people *not* related to me. People who bought into this fairy tale without criticism, without judgment. Objective points of view. A small win of sorts. Plus, if I could sway some votes my way, it would totally be worth it.

"Thanks," I said. "I'm honestly excited to talk about him."

With a word hanging off my tongue, another classmate, Madelyn, entered. I turned and greeted her with my eyes. Her lips parted into a wide smile.

"So, he lives in Portland?" Timothy said, breaking the connection with the girl. He slid farther to the front of his seat to convey his interest, leaning toward me as he balanced himself on the desk. "That's so wild."

Nodding, I replied, "Yeah. In fact, I just saw him the other day."

Timothy didn't need to know that I worked at Sir's food cart. I couldn't give him that information. That was like broadcasting where the Batcave was and displaying each gadget in Batman's utility belt.

"Are you talking about your superhero relative?" Madelyn asked, aiming for a desk within earshot. She moved her bangs behind her ear and smiled.

"I am," I said. "Anything you want to know?"

C'mon. Ask me anything.

Madelyn sat down in the chair, leaned in toward me, and said, "Not particularly. I just find it fascinating." She spread her belongings across the desk, scattering them with little regard.

Another vote for Team Tsinelas.

The rest of the kids in the class (only a handful) leaned forward as well, joining in on the conversation, if only as spectators. Who knew if they thought the video was faked? For now, I had their attention. It was mine to hold, so I had to play this right.

"It is pretty wild," I said. "Sometimes he's supposed to come over for dinner, but then he doesn't show for some reason."

"Some reason?" said Timothy. "He's out fighting crime."

Then we laughed.

As we shared a moment, Clint entered. Because of course he did. He had that timing in his favor.

He picked up on it instantly. Again, he was Clint, and everything went his way. A car dealership in the family, Hall of Fame quarterback, popularity. Spidey-Senses?

Just flat out take me out!

"You talking about this so-called superhero?" he said, his tone condescending. His eyes moved from Madelyn to Timothy, to the other kids, and then to me.

My body tensed as he neared me. I just sat waiting for something to happen.

"You honestly think this nerd is related to a superhero?" Clint's body puffed up, the very image of a grizzly bear showing his superiority. "Or is it the fact that he's delusional and honestly believes that superheroes exist?"

I turned toward the front of the room, the nerves inside me twitching with every second that passed. I began to feel uneasy, my body temperature rising to enough of a degree that I might burst into flames.

Clint's stare hit me, and deep down, I wished that Sensei was here to prove Clint wrong. To knock him silly with a ratty slipper or take him out with a pair of microphone nunchucks. Anything just to make him stop.

But he wasn't here, and instead, I heard a chorus from Lola and Ginessa saying, "I told you so, I told you so," in my head.

"We do," Timothy said, and my attention returned. "Don't you think it's rad?"

"*Suuuuure*," said Clint, drawing out the word sarcastically. "If this *quote, unquote* superhero is real."

Of course he's real!

I couldn't restrain myself, screaming internally until my throat hurt! My eyes floated toward Clint, who was glaring back at me. Swallowing hard, I shook my head.

"We all know that Victor is a loser." He paused, urging me with his focused gaze. "He's a nobody, and for him *not* to be a nobody, he dreamed up this story about this imaginary superhero." Clint was a district attorney targeting Timothy like a juror. He laughed and then shook his head.

My temperature had spilled over the top, and I was fuming. Like Johnny Storm, the Human Torch, I was ready to ignite myself into a flame. I needed to reel my emotions in. I had to control myself. But how?

"He could have a superhero relative," said Timothy with a playful smile, combating Clint's skepticism. "Portland's weird like that."

Instantly, the heat building inside began to cool.

"Listen to how silly that sounds," Clint replied. "A superhero relative in an obviously faked video. It was so generic. A crowd in Pioneer Square? Anyone could have put that video together."

I glared at my nemesis.

"It wasn't faked," I muttered.

Clint turned to me, his eyes zeroing in on mine. I was trapped in my desk with no place to hide.

"You're just overcompensating," he accused, then stopped, waiting for me to respond.

Suddenly, my eyes whitened, and I was Storm from X-Men, controlling the temperature around us to the point that a bolt of lightning shot through the classroom's window and flung Clint across the room. Clint hit the wall hard and then his body slid to the floor. Those in attendance watched in both horror and amazement. Suddenly, their collective heads whipped over in my direction. I was back to normal.

"Aren't you?" he asked, attempting to engage me in something more than a stare-down.

I didn't engage. Instead, I stayed silent—my best point of defense was to avoid, avoid, avoid (was that one of Storm's superpowers?)—long enough for Miss Francis to disrupt the thick tension when she entered.

"Good afternoon, everyone," she announced, her voice halting the near conflict.

Clint's attitude changed in an instant, his intimidating demeanor transforming into something I had never seen. Normally, he would stay quiet and return to his seat. But this time, he was . . . obedient. He was. . . nice. Respectful. And playing along. Totally unlike Clint.

"Good afternoon, Miss Francis," he said, full of life, and then found his desk.

More kids filed in, each collecting his or her seat. There was some slight chatter amongst them. Bart entered and brushed past me. He and Clint high-fived—*SLAP!*—loud enough for me to hear.

The slight rush inside subsided into the underbelly of fear and insecurity. It was good while it lasted. My plan now shifted to sitting quietly and working on the project, tweaking it as needed.

The time hit the top of the hour and Miss Francis counted the students.

"Good afternoon," she said to the entire room. "I hope everyone had a great day and night since the last time we were together." She waited for a response but there was nothing. I stared at my desk, counting the groove marks on the wooden desktop, hoping that they would magically swirl into some message that unlocked the key to getting out of this predicament. "Today, we're going to work on our papers. Does anyone have any questions?"

Behind me, there was some slight giggling. Just hearing them made me squirm, their voices loud and obnoxious. I let it get to me, to the point where I began doubting what I was doing. Hearing Lola and Ginessa's voices was a sign. And I almost believed the video was faked, even though, deep down, I knew that it had occurred exactly how it looked. But the paper was so good!

"I have a question," blurted Clint.

"Yes, Clint," Miss Francis pointed in his direction. A group of heads, including mine, turned to face him.

Clint cut me a quick glance and smiled out the side of his mouth.

"I think Victor's project sounds amazing," he said. One classmate nearby clapped.

My heartbeat instantly tripled. My insecurity was now so fragile that every word was like walking over a rickety suspension bridge between two cliffs. Was he just jealous because my topic would get the most votes? Where was he going with this?

"So amazing," continued Clint, "that instead of just talking about it, I think he should bring Sensei in."

The brakes on my racing heart screeched across the pavement of 'what the halo-halo' lane. What did he mean, bring Sensei in? I'd already asked him! Plus, this wasn't a show-and-tell presentation (trust me, I'd thought about that!); it was a 'just go up to the front of the room and speak until the time expired' presentation. Kill time with 'uh' and 'um' and 'er' until the teacher cut you off and told you to sit down. The fact that I'd found a topic worth talking about was a bonus. But I fully intended to fill the gaps with awkward utterances until my time ran out. Maybe dazzle them with some cool stories about us. I mean, who in the world wanted to present in front of the class?

"Don't you think that's a good idea?" Clint prodded the other teens. "Oh, and Victor? I was wrong. The video isn't fake. My bad."

Some of the kids were on board with the decision, joining the lone clapper and hooting at the idea.

Even though the most popular kid in school was giving me what I wanted, I couldn't breathe, and my eyes widened like they never had before. The need to check my pulse to ensure I wasn't dead occurred to me, but the fact that this was happening in real time proved I was alive and well. . .for the meantime, at least.

"I mean, since it was such a big hit with the class." Clint turned and pointed to Bart with his thumb. "Bart's bringing in some chocolate samples. So, I just thought it would be cool to make this kind of a show-and-tell, that's all. Who wouldn't want to meet a real-life superhero?" Clint shrugged and an impish smile grew across his lips. "I mean, I'd ask my grandfather to come in but," he dropped his head with sharp aptitude, "he's dead."

Now he's laying it on super thick. He was one comment away from bringing in a spirit board and getting the class to summon his dead grandfather.

At once, the entire classroom of kids, including Miss Francis, turned to me. I had never seen so many eyeballs at the same time. Most of the kids wore excited expressions as if this could potentially happen.

"Victor, you only have to present the paper you've written," Miss Francis said. "And Bart, you're not required to bring in samples either."

One girl audibly groaned at the last part.

I hadn't moved; I was still in shock from the request, my pulse breaking world records. The suspension bridge was going to break, and I slouched into my seat.

"Uh," I muttered, trying to stall for time. "Um . . ." Now, if only the time would run out and I could bail out of here like The Flash. "Er . . ."

With heavy stares upon me, I fidgeted, and the pupils of my eyes darted around the room. Which superhero power could make me disappear?

"I don't know if that's possible," I dismissed the question with a quick shake of my head. "He's very busy, he has, uh, things to do."

"Right . . ." said Clint. "The least you could do is ask."

"Yeah," Madelyn said. "Just ask him."

"What could it hurt?" Timothy added.

"C'mon," shouted someone else.

"The fans have spoken," said Bart.

I licked my top lip. Swallowing hard for the umpteenth time, my mind raced in every direction, my gut buried in my heels. There wasn't anyone coming to save me. I was in this alone.

I knew I'd already asked Sir, but the stakes were higher. If I could only convince him to appear, it would change everything.

"Class," said Miss Francis, somewhat ending the likelihood of her students starting a planned celebration like a city street parade or international breakdance battle. "If Victor wants to ask Sensei Tsinelas to come in, he will, but let's leave it up to—"

"I'll do it!"

Then, in my head, I said, *Again*.

HE CAN SEE RIGHT THROUGH ME!

I sat in my seat for the rest of the class, tap, tap, tapping my foot nonstop until Miss Francis dismissed us. By the end of it, my leg was in pain, tingling from the continuous motion. And no, it didn't give me the superpower of electricity.

I tried to bolt as soon as class was over, but Miss Francis called my name. I froze.

"Can I talk to you for a second?"

The kids were filing to the door, and I slinked over to Miss Francis's desk, waiting until the final person exited.

She stood from her seat and closed the door.

"Have a seat," she said. Miss Francis then pulled her chair out from behind her desk and placed it in front of me. "How are you doing?" She leaned toward me, propping her elbows onto her knees.

"Fine," I said. "Why do you ask?"

"Well, I want to make sure you're okay with what happened in class."

Dismissing her with a quick shrug, I said, "Yeah. I think he would be a great addition to my presentation."

She pressed her lips into a straight line.

"Kind of seemed like you were pressured."

Shaking my head, I said, "Regardless. It would be cool to show him off."

Miss Francis pinched out a smile.

"Would you like for me to look at your paper first?"

I did my best to hide my panic. What I really needed was to get to the food cart so I could ask Sir to appear in class.

"I don't think so," I replied. "I promise it'll be fine."

Miss Francis displayed some hesitancy. All the while, my toe began to tap in anxiousness again.

"I trust that it will," she said. Then she sat up and lengthened her torso. "Okay. I'm just going to let you know that if you want me to take a look at your paper, I'm more than happy to."

"I appreciate that."

"And also," Miss Francis said, "you're not required to bring him in. Just remember that."

I nodded in understanding and then I was gone.

I told Ginessa that I had to work at the last minute, so when we arrived at our usual stop to walk home, I apologized for leaving her for the rest of the night.

"I'm going to head straight to work," I explained. "You gonna be okay to walk home by yourself?" I glanced down the road to where we normally headed, then returned to Ginessa.

"It's no big deal," Ginessa nodded. "As long as you've requested the day of the picnic off, we're making progress." She smiled. "Plus, I'm going to make a practice flan tonight with Lola." Then she lifted her nostrils to the air as if smelling the dessert and grinned. Her cheeks rounded out as her smile grew wider. After she took in her imaginary aroma, she returned to me. "Have fun at work."

If only.

"Thanks, I will," I said. "Just text me if you need anything."

I walked the opposite direction to Sir's cart, down the sidewalk until I reached the end of the block, where I turned the corner and twisted my upper body to see if Ginessa was still visible behind me. In the clear, I picked up the pace and booked it to the block of food carts. I ran faster than I'd ever run before.

Conjuring up a superpower, my human speed transformed into something extraordinary. I was running so fast my legs were blurry, and it looked as if I had grown extra limbs. In my mind, I knew I wasn't running any faster, but it felt like it.

When Filipino Feast was within sight, I slowed my pace to a walk.

A couple was at the window talking to Sir, who was pointing to the large menu on the outside of the cart. With each point, Sir explained what the dish comprised. He was so animated in his demeanor, his hands moving around in circles and sudden motions.

I moved into Sir's line of vision until we caught each other's stare. His eyes flashed, and he acknowledged me with a nod. I entered the cart and waited with jittery anxiousness for Sir to finish the transaction.

He returned to his customers and after they placed their orders, he slid in next to me to whip up the meals. Around me came rustling noises alongside the fryer's oil sizzling, revving with each item thrown into the scalding vat.

Szzzzzzz...Szzzzzzz...

"What you doing here?" he asked. "You don't work today."

I sucked in my bottom lip, my gaze darting from the customers to the fryer and back.

"I wanted to ask you something," I replied, short and sweet.

"Must be important." He finished up the order and returned to the window.

Deep down, I was sweating something terrible.

Szzzzzzz...Szzzzzzz...

All the while, I stood, bouncing on the balls of my toes, desperately trying to dissipate some nervous energy. I teetered side to side in nervousness, and my eyebrows knitted.

The hairs on the nape of my neck raised, and my insecurity was on high alert.

"Thank you." Sir slid the containers to the couple. "Come back again." He watched the couple leave before he spun back around to find me.

He jutted his chin.

"What you wanna ask?"

Finally.

I couldn't manage to keep eye contact with him, and my hands trembled, so I clasped them together. He picked up on my behavior instantly.

"You okay?" said Sir. "You look distressed." For some reason, I couldn't speak. Was I that nervous? Was I out of line by even asking again? Was he going to flip me over like he did with that robber? When the silence became uncomfortable, he said, "Have you eaten?"

"No," I answered, drumming up that slight bit of courage. "That's not why I'm here."

Sir's eyes narrowed.

Leaning in closer, he said, "You not working. You not hungry. What's up?"

He can see right through me!

"I just... I need to ask you something."

"You say that already," he said. "Ask."

"I wanted to ask you again about reconsidering," I said. "About coming to my school?"

Sir fell into a trance, his gaze becoming empty, distant.

"Please," I said. "I wouldn't ask if I didn't think it was important."

"Covering up your lie not important."

"Me not getting my butt kicked is," I said.

He scanned me up and down, glossing over every inch of my body. He twirled his finger in the air, gesturing for me to spin around.

I did, and when I faced him again, he said, "But you fine."

"Please?"

Sir stood in silence, broken only by the low purr of frying oil behind us, and I could sense that he was thinking about it. Maybe hearing about my getting hurt would change his mind. It did seem that when someone was actually involved, he acted—Pioneer Square incident, the mugging, the food cart robbery—but with the tip jar, he let things go. Could that be the trigger?

"Victor," he began. "Why you not learn lesson from family tree? You try to take easy way out and look where it get you. Now you lie so people like you? People won't like you for that. They like what in here." He patted his heart with his open hand. "You a smart kid. Big future ahead of you. I don't want to be responsible for straying you away."

I was almost at my wit's end, ready to concede, but I tried one more thing. I threw out a *Hail Mary*. If this didn't work, I was ready to give up.

"Forget my dilemma for one second. Let's talk about you and what you mean to people like me." A background orchestra began playing in my head, softly, underneath my monologue. "You whipped your slipper at that mugger in front of me," I said. "In front of a few of us. Like it was nothing. And then you fought off that burglar who was trying to rob the food cart. It was *awesome!*"

Pausing with a flair for the dramatics, my tongue grazed across my upper lip. The symphony was now passing its slow second movement and entering its third, a quick tempo complementing this awkward exchange.

"And the video? It's already out there for people to see. People already think there's a superhero out there looking over us. Maybe it's time you came out and identified yourself. You keep saying you got lucky, but I'm telling you otherwise." I looked around the area. People were ordering from food carts, enjoying the day without a worry on their minds. "People who witnessed your heroics, who saw this video, would think otherwise as well."

"I don't like that video being online," Sir said. "Too much attention."

"So, you're admitting it's you?"

He ignored me.

"How do I erase?"

The symphony's final movement then hit.

"Don't you see? It wasn't a coincidence that I witnessed the tsinelas throw and you breaking up that burglary. Or that someone caught this other event on video. All of this was fate. Me loving superheroes. Me taking a job here. You having the best adobo in town which brought people to your cart. Someone ordering at the exact same time a crime happened? It's not a coincidence. It can't be!"

I wasn't sure if my plea was going to work.

"It just can't," I said, suddenly becoming emotional. Sniffling, I muttered, "It just can't."

"Ay," said Sir. "Susmaryosep." His face warped in every direction. A sigh here. A deep rolling of his eyes there. Then I thought he mean mugged me.

"Fine," he finally surrendered. "I will come to your school."

KNOWING IS HALF THE BATTLE

After two other practice flans, Ginessa was finally ready to test one.

When I arrived at the cafeteria, I took the seat across from Ginessa. She was sitting with two other kids who had also volunteered themselves. I immediately noticed that they were the same girls who were hanging out with her during the Italian food mishap. Thinking about that situation suddenly caused me to scan the area for Clint and Bart.

Before I could fall too heavily into my head, Ginessa asked her friends if they remembered me. Elena smiled and Denise nodded.

The last time they saw me I was wearing my lunch. I only hoped that I would cast a different impression on them. I smiled politely.

"Good seeing you two," I said. "Are you excited about this as I am?"

The practice flan sat in separate Tupperware containers in the center of us.

"We sure are," said Denise, rubbing her small hands together. "We always love your family's cooking."

Elena, on the other hand, just sat with anxious eyes.

"I wanted impartial testers," said Ginessa.

"Good idea," I said nonchalantly, my eyes subconsciously observing my surroundings. "Where are they?" I said jokingly. "The impartial testers."

Ginessa's brow raised slightly.

"Seriously, can we do this?"

"Sorry," I said. "Let's do it."

With a pen in her hand and a notebook in front of her, Ginessa sat positioned to take notes on what she needed to do to improve the dessert. She'd clearly worked hard on it. It looked perfect. It smelled perfect.

"I followed the recipe to a T," she said. "The first time I wanted to try it by myself. Out of pride. To prove I could do it. But it didn't turn out like I hoped." She pouted. "The second time, well, I don't know what happened. But this time, Lola supervised, so I'm hoping it tastes all right."

"Don't be so hard on yourself," said Elena. "I'm sure it tastes delicious."

"Yeah," Denise added. "Cooking isn't the easiest thing to do. One time, I tried . . ." and then my mind drifted.

As her friends gave Ginessa moral support, I imagined a scene where Lola and Ginessa were side by side, training in some unusual choreography between sensei and student.

Mister Miyagi and Daniel.

Master Shifu and Po.

And who could forget Master Splinter and the Teenage Mutant Ninja Turtles?

Lots of screaming occurred too.

"Egg!" Then a punch.

"Vanilla!" Then a kick.

"Bake!" Then a combination kick-punch.

No matter what I tried, I couldn't get what transpired out of my head. I mean, Sir was coming to my school! But I had to focus for Ginessa's sake.

I returned to the flan and the three girls.

Rubbing my palms together, I said, "I'm excited." And I was.

Ginessa pulled out four forks from her backpack and handed them out.

"Okay," said Ginessa nervously, her forehead wrinkling. "I want you all to be honest."

Elena and Denise nodded. They were ready just like I was.

"Of course," I promised, digging into the flan and lifting the plastic fork to my mouth as the texture melted off the utensil.

My eyes closed as I slowly chewed. I savored the taste of the caramel-flavored brown sugar. Swallowing, I subtly winced. The bite was somewhat liquid in consistency, unlike the flans that I'd had in the past, which had a gelatin feel to them. Something was wrong.

My eyebrows drew together, and I licked my upper lip.

Denise chewed while wiping her mouth with a napkin.

"The flavor is definitely there," I said. "But I feel like you didn't cook it long enough. The inside was a little runny."

Elena nodded and said, "But it's good though."

Ginessa frowned with a look of disappointment on her face.

"I knew it," she whispered. She sighed noticeably. "Not solid enough?" Together, the three of us nodded. "Lola thought it could cook for a few more minutes, but I swear I followed the recipe line by line this time." Her voice trailed off and she quietly berated herself, mouthing something only she could hear. "I should've listened to her."

"It's okay," I consoled, placing my fork on the tabletop. "You're still learning. You're not going to be at Mom or Lola's level yet. So don't be so hard on yourself. Everything else is good. The flavors are all there but the texture isn't. It should be an easy fix."

"Yeah," said Denise. "Just a little longer."

"Noted." She jotted some words down in her notebook, the same one covered in the advanced math problems, and thanked me.

I scanned the page, my head tilting to the side, but decided not to mention the mysterious notepad. Instead, I asked, "What did the other ones taste like?"

"One was way too sweet. And then there was the one that we could eat like a pizza. I still don't know what happened there." She laughed out loud, and I could tell that her mood was better.

"I can't even imagine," Elena said.

"Well, practice makes perfect," I said. I placed my palm delicately on top of Ginessa's hand, and with a loving gesture, I consoled, "Hey, I'm sorry about not listening to your story on the train about the theft." A partial smile escaped the side of my mouth. "It's just that my mind has been consumed by this paper. I've been working on it like crazy. And now I'm dreaming about it. I guess I really want it to be voted the best."

"The one that I disapprove of?" she teased. Smiling, I nodded. "So, you're still going with your idea."

"Looks like it," I said, attempting to dismiss the conversation.

It worked because she suddenly turned to Elena and Denise and caught them up about the assignment. Elena's eyes widened as if she couldn't believe I was writing it as well.

Turning to me, Ginessa asked, "How is it coming along?" She leaned in closer, her eyes filled with elusive interest, a nice distraction from a failed flan attempt.

"Let me tell you . . . "

And I did, starting from the beginning, from the slipper incident to the Pioneer Square protest to the attempted burglary to what happened in class, all the way up to the discussion with Sir and how he finally agreed to come.

"He's coming?"

"Today."

"Why would he—"

Out of nowhere, Clint and Bart sidled up next to me. I didn't see them at first; their shadows appeared over me like a dark mass suddenly manifesting in a haunted ghost hunt.

"What do we have here?" Clint asked in a sing-song manner. The hairs on my neck rose, stiff on command. Like sharp quills. Totally un-Sonic the Hedgehog-like. Hearing his voice instantly set me on high alert.

Clint reached in between us and picked up my container of flan. He examined the yellowish dessert from all angles, rotating it in his hands as his head cocked to his right. The flan jiggled from side to side. Luckily, it was confined to the Tupperware.

My imagination ran wild. What if I stood up and pushed the dessert into his face? He'd be covered in flan and would feel the same way I'd felt with the spaghetti. Maybe he would learn a lesson and we'd suddenly become friends. At the end, one of us could give a public service announcement to the at-home audience like G.I. Joe did after every episode. "Now you know. And knowing is half the battle." Or what if I grabbed him by the collar, raised him above my head, shook him to death? Sadly . . .

Sniffing the container, he said, "It smells like milk and eggs."

Bart leaned in and took a whiff.

"I smell caramel. Maybe some brown sugar."

"Did you make this for us?" asked Clint.

I frowned, and all I could think of was how the flan would somehow end up all over me. Like a villain being sprayed with Spider-Man's web fluid, sticky from head to toe. The situation was reminiscent of every other encounter with Clint. I was a nerd, and Clint was on top of the world. Why would anything change now? Who in the world was I to ever—

"*I* made it," Ginessa said, her teeth grinding. Her voice came out of nowhere, and I swore it sounded super deep and guttural. It was so commanding that Denise sat back like she was hiding from view.

Ginessa stood to her feet, her once relaxed manner now gone, and pointed directly at Clint. She looked like Bruce Banner transforming into Hulk at this moment. Hulk wearing a baro't saya. Clint was nearly two feet taller than Ginessa, but he stumbled back a step regardless.

"And no, I *didn't* make it for you."

"Oh." He returned the flan to the table and then gave her some space. Bart followed suit. "I wasn't aware that you made it," he said with a brittle voice. "I apologize."

My eyes widened. What was happening? She had him at her mercy. In my head, the disembodied voice in Mortal Kombat was screaming, "Finish him!"

Clint and Bart exchanged looks and then Bart elbowed him. Clint turned his attention toward my direction, his demeanor more manageable.

"So, is Sensei chinchilla coming or what?"

Tsinelas.

"I don't know," I said, suddenly with inspiration, knowing that he was, in fact, coming. "Is he?"

"That's what I thought," said Clint, leaning in closer. "Because superheroes don't exist. Quit lying. Didn't your mother teach you not to lie?"

I'd suddenly had enough, partly because he brought up Mom, and heat rose in my cheeks. I erupted out of my skin and the Wolverine in me came out.

I thought I was fantasizing, but my fists were clenched—the unattended fingernails digging deep into my skin—and I lunged at Clint. I was much smaller than him, so I hardly made a dent in his armor of evil.

He did stumble back one step though. He grabbed my shirt's collar, tightened his grip, and stared down at me.

The kids around us stopped to watch, and it almost felt like the noise disappeared. I could feel his energy swallowing me up, and I closed my eyes to brace myself for what would happen next.

Before any teachers could come to my defense, I heard a voice.

"How is that scholarship?" asked Ginessa slyly. "Still getting it?"

There was suddenly a release from my body. My shirt loosened and returned to its normal fit around my torso. I opened my eyes, and Clint was no longer in my orbit.

"Um . . . still on par," said Clint, stammering over his words. His eyes quickly darted around the cafeteria. I followed his line of sight. One teacher was surveying the crowd. Another was cautiously peering in our direction.

Ginessa's gaze stayed locked on Clint until he backed off.

I slowly exhaled, and my eyes danced between Ginessa and Clint, observing what on God's earth was happening. Elena and Denise sat still like they were frozen in time. This hint of weakness and vulnerability in Clint was all due to my kid sister standing up to him. Standing up to the most popular boy in school.

Like she was his kryptonite.

ONE AND ONLY SUPERHERO

Later, I greeted Sir at the front door. Getting the most votes was in the bag, and I told myself that if I won, I would never speak about this again. I would have achieved what I'd wanted, and Sir could go back to running his food cart the way he'd intended.

Rounding the corner and with Sir in tow, I approached the classroom. And to be honest, it looked more like *I* was the superhero than Sir.

It was mainly because I knew my way around the school. But still! Who was I to let this small technicality ruin my mood? Every superhero series always had one episode where the least likely person to solve the case did so. Think Wonder Twins' Zan and Jayna and their alien monkey, Gleek. Nobody knew what their role in the series was until that one time. This wasn't any different. At least that was how I looked at it.

The walk, however, was taking longer than usual because Sir found the lockers fascinating, saying that maybe he could put one in the cart to use as storage.

All I was thinking was, *Is this what superhero-ing is really about?* I knew they had secret identities and all, but did they really just do mundane things when they weren't out saving the world?

I didn't recall Batman and Robin killing time at the laundromat's pool table while they waited for the dryer to finish its cycle. And did superhero tights take longer to dry? Was there ever a time when the Bat Signal rang out and Batman was like, "Dude, I still have twenty minutes left on the dryer cycle."

Or Hawkman polishing his harness made from the Nth metal that gave him his power of flight while he waited for a Banquet TV dinner to finish cooking in the microwave?

Was this really a thing?

Sir wasn't certain if he needed a lock and if so, whether a key or combination would be the answer. A key could get lost but perhaps it would go nicely around a necklace? Superman had the letter "S" so maybe it could represent a symbol or something?

"Add some mystery," he said. "People wonder what key unlocks." Then he giggled, ending with, "It unlocks taste buds."

I rolled my eyes and chuckled. I explained that he probably wouldn't need to lock it since the locker would be in the food cart.

"Oh," he uttered. "Right." He nodded. "Plus, I always lock up cart. Especially after you-know-what."

I knew exactly what he was talking about.

"Where's your locker?" he asked.

I pointed down the hall.

"In a different wing," I answered.

He gave me a look, almost as if he wanted me to show him, but when I said that it resembled the other lockers he simply nodded, and that was that.

"They're not like the food carts where each is unique to the owner," I said. "I guess some people decorate the outsides but mine is pretty basic."

He stood motionless as if he was stalling or something, like he changed his mind. That was when I realized that he didn't want to be here, and I felt guilty for dragging him into my mess.

I gestured down the hall with my lips and we trudged on until we found the classroom. As we neared the room, my excitement began to explode within. I couldn't believe this was about to go down.

We entered.

In my mind, Sir's presence was so dominant that a gust of wind traveled throughout the class and caused whiplash across the first row of kids. A loud *WHOOSHING* noise complemented the motion.

The room full of kids, all postured in their respective seats, watched in amazement as I rushed to the front of the classroom, jamming my fists into my hips. I gestured behind me where Sir was standing.

"Here he is," I announced. "The one and only superhero, Sensei Tsinelas."

A huge greeting erupted when the first few rows of kids stood to cheer.

Miss Francis, sitting at her desk in the front of the room, stood and quieted the crowd.

"Okay, everyone," she said. "Let's not get too rowdy." Turning to me, she nodded. "Victor, I just want to remind you *again* that this wasn't a show-and-tell." Her eyes grazed over to Sir and she smiled. "Thank you for coming but it wasn't necessary."

"I said I would bring him," I almost sang. "So here he is!"

"I understand," she said.

Her lackluster interest sent mixed signals. Maybe she was in awe of his status. Not many people of this caliber paraded through the school, much less her classroom. On one occasion, a retired mayor did a talk, but I think that was all.

Sir bowed to various kids who'd made eye contact with him. They didn't seem to know what to do, as some bowed back and others hid their smiles. I just assumed they were impressed. Emotions were weird like that.

Just then, a girl entered, prancing to her desk as she passed.

"Hey!" she said excitedly upon seeing Sir.

This was how you responded when you met a real-li—

"I love your adobo!" she said. To her friend sitting in the front row, she gestured to Sir. "This is who I was talking about. He makes the best pork adobo in Portland."

Sir smiled.

"Thank you," he said. "You come later. I give you discount. Just say you saw me here."

Clint and Bart laughed.

"A superhero," mocked Clint. Then, as if his pitch raised a notch, he said, "Let's see him do some cool things."

"Yeah," added Bart. "Kick in that brick wall."

They encouraged the other kids to join in. Some did, those who'd already been psyched about his appearance. But Miss Francis quickly stopped the slight ruckus before it could turn into a full-blown riot.

"Victor, please have a seat," said Miss Francis. "Before you begin, I'd like to talk to Sensei in the hall really quick."

Miss Francis led Sir out of the classroom. The door closed. For a second, I wondered what they were going to discuss. Maybe some extra appearances afterward when they discovered how awesome he was? Maybe some autograph sessions and photo ops? Or maybe she was confirming the discount coupon at Filipino Feast? I shrugged.

I was so lost in myself that I didn't even notice Clint starting a chant.

"Sensei, Sensei, Sensei." The chant caught on in an instant and shortly thereafter, most of the class had joined. "Sensei, Sensei, Sensei!"

The chant jarred me back to the present. I looked around and when I made eye contact with Clint, he smirked.

"Here's your chance," he said. "Give your presentation. This is what you wanted, right?"

My eyes drifted to the door. I could see Miss Francis and Sir in deep discussion through the thick, glass window.

"But, they're still in the hall," I said.

Now that it was getting close to showtime I started to feel the pressure and wondered if what I was doing was the right choice, as most of the paper was made up. Subconsciously, I was hoping that Sir would come in and save me.

"Just go ahead and start," said Bart. "They could be out there for a while."

I wasn't sure what to do at this moment. Until the chant of "Sensei, Sensei, Sensei," picked back up. My mouth started watering and when I swallowed the excess saliva, I closed my eyes. The sounds of the many voices around me, especially from those who believed in Sensei, encouraged me to go on. I had to do it for them as well as myself.

"Sensei, Sensei, Sensei."

"Sensei, Sensei, Sensei!"

"Sensei, Sensei, Sensei!"

For the most part, I was able to restrain myself.

But then, Clint said, "What're you waiting for, loser?"

The comment set me over the edge and I rose from my seat.

Turning to him, I said, "Fine, I'll do it!"

The cheers of my classmates solidified my decision. I would show them.

I walked to the front of the class, exhaled deeply and then began.

"Sensei Tsinelas," I said, "relocated to the Portland area from the Midwest, where he opened up a successful Filipino-based food cart." The kids were hanging on my every word, so I continued. "I first met Sensei when I took a job at his food cart. He was . . ."

I took the next minute or so introducing the life of Sensei Tsinelas and how my family and I fit into it. I outlined our heroics, relaying the paper I'd written. Every single word. Even though it wasn't in a final draft's form, it was pretty detailed.

A few of the kids in the front row cut quick glances toward each other. One classmate in my peripheral contained laughter behind her hand.

Clint, Bart, and the other jocks were slapping each other's shoulders, bending over in amusement.

I turned to look out into the hall. Sir and Miss Francis were deep into conversation. His expression was vigorous, like he was entertaining her with stories of past prowess.

I pushed on, telling the story that had occurred at Pioneer Place, the large mall near Pioneer Square.

"When we approached the doors," I read, "a crook was running out the mall's exit.

"'Get back here!' a security guard screamed.

"The guard was chasing the thief, dodging shoppers who were milling around the entrance and in front of the building.

"It all happened so quickly and I froze, but not Sensei.

"He extended his arms, his palms pointing out toward the thief. Mahjong tiles hidden in his sleeves shot out from his hands like lasers and landed in front of the criminal, splaying out in front of his feet. The thief didn't even see them coming."

"Victor?" interjected Miss Francis. She was one foot into the room and one foot out. Her voice startled me, bringing me out of my groove. I turned to address her.

"Yeah?"

"What're you doing?" she asked. "I didn't say you could start."

"Oh . . ." I said, and then my gaze darted to where Clint and Bart were sitting. Almost like I needed their approval.

Miss Francis's attention moved to Sir, who raised his hand to stop her. He mouthed, "It's okay," and the teacher cautiously nodded.

What were they talking about?

"Well, I guess you can carry on," she said, and then she closed the door and continued talking to Sir.

And so I did.

"In one quick motion, the shoplifter stepped on the Mahjong tiles and the tiles' ivory coating created a slick layer, similar to a cartoon grease spot, which caused the shoplifter's foot to kick up high in front of him and his body to fall backward.

"The spectators in attendance were both shocked and amazed at the superhero ability exhibited from Sensei Tsinelas.

"As for the shoplifter, it was like watching an amateur ice skater on the rink. It was incredible. If there were judges around, he wouldn't get higher than a three, maybe four for difficulty.

"Mall security apprehended the criminal while the shoppers, led by me and my enthusiasm, applauded Sensei."

I read the rest of the paper, and when I finished, I addressed the class. I'd never seen so many enlarged eyes staring at me at once. All so impressed, shocked, and jealous at the same time. In fact, the kids were speechless.

Just then, Miss Francis and Sir entered the room. Sir found a spot in the corner of the room and the teacher returned to her desk.

"That was the most bogus thing I'd ever heard," Clint said. "Clyde and Brad?" His shoulders bounced up and down a tad, like he was holding in his laughter.

"Yeah," added Bart. "I thought we were supposed to write about our family heritage. Not about a bunch of obviously made-up stories involving a chef. Some of those stories weren't even realistic."

"And us, apparently," Clint chimed in. Tapping Bart's shoulder, he said, "Don't forget about Clyde and Brad."

Even though I knew my paper was made up, my world suddenly began to blur. I wasn't expecting this reaction. The thought of winning best project had consumed me.

Bart shook his head.

Clint dropped his chin.

"Are you two even related?" some girl in the back said.

My heartbeat started racing and I felt nauseous. I went too far.

"Of course," I stammered. "We, uh, we're third cousins. Wait . . ."

"What?" asked Clint. "You just said you two were second cousins once removed."

I turned to Sir. He was quiet. I tried to make eye contact, but he wouldn't even look at me.

"Sensei?"

A tight-lipped smile escaped Sir's otherwise serious conduct. He shot a glance to Miss Francis, who stood disappointingly.

"Want to show them some cool stuff?" I asked. By now, I was sweating. From my pits to my forehead. "I was just warming them up. You're the real star. Maybe you can fling your slipper into the crowd?"

Sir awkwardly chuckled. He cleared his throat.

"Victor was, uh, just trying to make joke of presentation," he said. "He a comedian. Like Jo Koy."

A joke! What?

"Everybody knows superheroes don't exist." He shrugged, his jovial demeanor cutting the tension in the room. "I just a chef." He showed his palms to the room. "See, nothing special about me."

A few kids, mostly football players, burst out laughing.

"No, you're not," I said. "You're much more than that!"

Ignoring me, he said calmly, "I'm the owner of Filipino Feast, not a superhero."

There was more ridicule, this time all around me.

It felt like my throat was closing on me, the dryness making my lips and mouth sticky. Before the situation could become too much, Miss Francis stepped in.

"Class," she said. "That's enough."

But it wasn't. Not for Clint at least.

"What a super failure," said Clint.

The entire class seemed to be laughing at me.

I closed my eyes, and suddenly I was Nightcrawler, teleporting into another dimension until I found myself in my bedroom—my safe space. There was no one there to judge me, and it was then that I could finally relax.

"I said that's enough!" said Miss Francis.

My eyes jolted open.

The ridicule lessened, with sporadic giggles and whispers going in and out of my subconscious until I couldn't take it any longer.

The pages slithered out of my hand as my grasp loosened. Miss Francis came around from her desk and retrieved them. I slowly panned toward her, my body shaking uncontrollably.

She started to read the paper to herself. I saw her eyebrows rise high on her forehead, and she slowly shook her head.

My gaze darted around the room. To Miss Francis. To Sir. And then into the classroom. Faces were laughing, kids were pointing, but for the most part the room was in shock.

Staring out into the room, my heartbeat still running rampant, I turned toward the door and ran out.

FORTRESS OF SOLITUDE

When Superman wanted to get away, he disappeared to the Fortress of Solitude. It was his inner sanctum, a place to be alone, far from civilization.

My fortress was my bedroom.

I barricaded myself here after the presentation.

Since Lola and Ginessa had been preparing for the picnic, I managed to avoid them for the most part, saying I was sick. A couple times I flat-out ignored them. One time, I conjured up my inner Sue Storm from the *Fantastic Four* and rendered myself invisible. I wasn't sure if it worked or if they just let me be. Whatever the case, I knew it wouldn't last.

Knock, knock.

"Victor?" The door creaked open enough for Lola to poke her head in. "I know you haven't been feeling up to it," she said. "But we really need to talk."

I'd already felt bad for lying about my life, and I didn't need another person I thought I could trust to betray me. That was how supervillains were made. Everyone close to me had warned me but all that mattered was being popular, if only for one day.

"I'm not in the mood," I said.

The door pushed open more and Ginessa stepped into the room.

"You need to get in the mood," she said. "Everyone's worried about you."

"What are you talking about?"

"We know the presentation didn't go well."

"Huh?"

"Your teacher called Lola," said Ginessa. "I thought it was my fault at first." She sat on the edge of the bed. Lola entered completely and found the chair by my desk.

Taking a deep breath, I sat up and wiped the days' worth of saliva from my lips. The taste of sleep breath nearly took me out like a rock of Kryptonite.

"Why would it be your fault?" My eyes narrowed and the presentation replayed in my head. "It was Sir's fault. If he only admitted that he was a superhero, this would've never happened."

"It wasn't your boss's fault," said Lola.

"He's the one that didn't—"

"Victor?" interrupted Lola. I instantly clammed up. "You made up the entire paper to appease your classmates."

"No, I didn't," I said. "Technically, I made up most of it because he wouldn't admit the amazing things he's done. He's real. All he had to do was . . ." My voice trailed off. Then, I said softly, "It doesn't matter."

Lola and Ginessa exchanged looks.

"Both Ginessa and I told you to write about our family," said Lola. "But you didn't listen."

"I did listen," I replied, my voice fragile and on the verge of cracking.

"Miss Francis told me you ran out," explained Lola. "She said that your paper was all about your boss and how he was a superhero with powers. There really wasn't anything about our family."

"It was because . . ."

I dropped my chin and thought about the presentation and the stories I'd written in the paper, thinking about which stories were true and which were not. I only witnessed two of the events, and I saw the grainy video, but the others? They could've happened.

What stories about our family were true?

"We think you need to talk to someone," said Lola. My head raised and my eyes found hers. "We're all just worried about you and this superhero obsession."

"But you two didn't . . ." I stopped short. I had nothing.

"I understand wanting to impress your classmates," Lola said. "And that would be okay if the topic was fiction. But why make up a story about your boss being a superhero?"

Because he's real, I thought. Or at least I thought he was. Now, I guess don't know.

She grazed my hand with her palm, rubbing it gently. I could feel her warmth and compassion on my skin.

"It's not healthy," she continued. Lola and Ginessa exchanged sympathetic looks. "Miss Francis would like for you to meet with her and a counselor."

"About what?" I muttered. "I know what I did was wrong."

"Well, for one, you haven't really talked about Mom and Dad," said Ginessa. "I've been tell—"

Lola cleared her throat—*ahem*—and Ginessa stopped.

"She just wants to know that you're okay . . . mentally," said Ginessa. "We all do."

Pinching my lips, I nodded. I stared into the duvet and my body began to loosen. I swallowed hard. They were right. I hadn't talked about how I felt and maybe I subconsciously blamed them for my situation. Then I remembered what Ginessa had said a moment ago.

"Why did you think it was your fault?" I asked her.

"Because I was helping Clint and Bart with their homework," she answered, her eyes darting anywhere but on me.

"You were helping them?"

My heart sank, and if there was ever a time when I felt more betrayed by Ginessa, this was it. Like Clint and Bart had conspired with everyone—Ginessa, Sir, the universe—to be against me.

"Why would you help them?" I asked. "They've made my life miserable from day one."

"That's why," she responded. "I hated seeing how they treated you, so I agreed to help them with their homework. So they'd stop picking on you."

Their scholarships. She'd asked about the scholarships in the cafeteria.

Her head lowered in shame.

"I guess I screwed up, too," she said. "I should have never gotten involved."

Ginessa lowered her chin to her chest and placed her palms over her face. She sniffled under her hands.

"You didn't screw up," I replied. "It's my fault. You were just looking out for me."

My stomach dropped. It was then I realized that everyone was fighting my battles but me. I was letting Mom and Dad down without even realizing it and my thoughts immediately went to them.

Two of my favorite memories took place at Pioneer Square. Many people congregated in the square to watch events, hang out, or witness the greatest spectacles. But my favorite memories were the family brick and the tree lighting.

The public square was one large area covered in bricks inscribed with all the citizens' names who'd donated to construct the forty thousand square-foot city block.

There was a brick that Dad had purchased for us. It read our last name and the date we'd "adopted" it. I remembered the time we saw the city install the brick in front of several onlookers and other donators.

It was one of the family's big accomplishments—an actual piece of history with our name on it. I always stared at the brick from afar whenever I was near the square. In the mornings and afternoons, when I boarded and stepped off the train, it didn't matter. My eyes just drew to it. I could have been staring at a different brick (they all looked the same from that distance), but I didn't care. It always made me smile.

The lighting of the seventy-five-foot Douglas fir Christmas tree was one of the biggest events in the city and thousands of residents and tourists ventured out on the day after Thanksgiving to celebrate and kickoff the Christmas season.

I had come to the tree lighting in the past with my family. It was a special time for me and one of the few that made me feel secure, safe, and loved.

The massive sing-along with those in attendance, the sounds of laughing and the random street performers parading around the block was a celebration for my eyes and ears.

Everybody who attended was there for the same reason: to celebrate with family and friends and enjoy the moment with other Portlanders and Pacific Northwesterners. To feel included, united in the spirit of the season, and share the same experience.

I missed Mom and Dad. Even though I had Lola and Ginessa, I felt alone when they died.

Lola and Ginessa's voices rang inside. Not with criticisms about me; rather, the happy times like Lola making food for us in the morning and Ginessa talking excitedly about the upcoming picnic. I thought about walking Ginessa to school on her first day. She was so excited to be in high school—to be an adult now, as she called it. Just like me. And I dismissed her, shaking my head as if it wasn't important.

When I finally snapped back to reality with Lola and Ginessa, I said, "This all happened because I'm the screwup. And I'm going to fix it."

TRUST ME, I'VE BEEN THERE

Before class, Miss Francis was standing alone in the hall.

"Victor," she said, a compassionate smile across her face. "Hang on a moment."

A classmate passed by and entered the room. Miss Francis nodded and then she returned to me.

"I want to talk to you about something."

"Sure," I said, stepping off to the side to accommodate the foot traffic.

I peeked inside, and on the board, it read: *Work on papers and presentations. Topics must be approved first.* There was random chatter, and in between the voices, I heard Clint. He was barking out some garbage like any other day. Laughter followed.

Instantly, my heart hurt from all the pain he caused me. The embarrassment and humiliation had derailed me, causing me to go to an unhealthy place. And all for what? To win best presentation? Did being popular really matter to me?

When we were alone and the last kid had entered the classroom, Miss Francis closed the door.

"You've been gone for a couple days," she said. "So I wanted to see how things were going."

I composed myself, inhaled, and responded, "Fine, I guess."

"You didn't seem fine after your presentation."

I wasn't fine. I got there, sort of, but being here was bringing back some bad memories.

"Yeah, I realized I shouldn't have fabricated my paper," I answered. Her face winced when I said fabricated, and I smirked. "Okay, I shouldn't have lied and made up all those stories. But I really wanted to win the most votes."

Pressing her lips into a thin line, she nodded. Like she understood where I was coming from and how important it was.

"If this was a creative writing course, it would've been perfect," she said. "But this is social studies."

I bit down on my bottom lip. *If only*, I thought.

"If I'm being honest, maybe you should consider taking some creative writing classes, since you've got such an interest in make-believe. But fiction aside, I thought it was well-written, so think about that."

I thought about the paper and then nodded.

"It would also give you a nice creative outlet to explore your imagination," she continued. "Put all that talent to good use."

"I'll look into that," I said. "Thank you for recommending it."

"So back to your paper," she said, her eyes narrowing. "Were any of the stories true?"

"Yes. The parts about my family." I smiled. I didn't realize I was doing it. "Maybe not exactly," I said. "I mean, the superhero stories with them weren't. Well, the gist was, is what I'm trying to say. I did have an uncle come visit during the holidays and the scene was similar to that in my paper."

"Well, that's good." She slowly nodded. "If you don't mind me asking, how did it get to the point that you'd fictionalize your paper? Was it really because you wanted to win the most votes?"

How? Where did I begin? I thought about telling her about the slipper incident that I witnessed. She already saw the video, so I didn't need to rehash that.

"Victor?"

"Sorry," I said. "You want the short version, or the long version?"

"I want the real version."

I briefly talked about my family, how I'd been ashamed of my culture and oftentimes punished my parents for my being born brown. Not like punishing physically but internally. Passive aggressively, I guessed. It wasn't anything they did per se; rather, it was something I'd built in my head a long time ago. A narrative I'd created. My own origin story. Then, the family tree project happened, and the villains of the world capitalized on my insecurity and fragility when all I wanted to do was ride out high school being a superhero-loving nerd. They confirmed why I felt this way. And so the cycle continued, only becoming worse as time progressed. But then I met Sir, and I became obsessed. I saw him as a way out. A way out of feeling this way, being made fun of, and finally erasing the family tree disaster. A way to somehow trick my mind into believing that I was okay. That I would be fine. That I, too, was in fact super.

"I see," she said, nodding gently as she glanced inside the classroom. I followed her gaze, and then our eyes met.

"If anything, all of this got me to this point, almost like the bullies' role, my parents' role, and Sir's role positioned me in this way. I was just tired of being the constant joke."

"No one wants to be the constant punchline," she said. She gestured to my shirt. "Is that why you're always sporting superhero shirts?"

I nodded and looked down at the plain, black Batman logo across my chest.

"The superhero scenarios are how I cope."

"Is Batman your favorite?"

"Superman is," I said. "Mainly because Superman is the greatest immigrant story ever. An alien who crash-landed in America's heartland—Smallville, Kansas—and was adopted by Jonathan and Martha Kent. He was forced to keep his identity secret . . . like his origins—"

"You mean how you want to keep your being Filipino secret?"

I guess.

"Something like that," I said. "But then when Clark is Superman, he's this beloved superhero that everyone relies on. Nobody cares or knows that he's an alien, an immigrant. Maybe I got carried away because I wanted to have the same feeling. I never *actually* thought superheroes existed before, well . . ." My voice trailed off and I shrugged.

"Sensei Tsinelas," said Miss Francis.

I nodded.

"Plus, maybe if there was a Superman, he could reverse time and bring my parents back."

That was the first time I'd said that out loud and the emotions hit me hard. My body weakened but then Miss Francis reached for me, her palm softly grazing my forearm.

"Unfortunately, you can't bring your mom and dad back," she said. "But you can learn to manage those feelings in a more productive way."

Nodding, I whispered, "I know." I was quiet for a minute, and before it became too painful for me, I said, "You probably can't relate to being the butt of jokes. You seem so well-liked and put-together."

"I don't know about all that," she replied with a short laugh. "But thank you for looking at me that way."

I didn't know what else to say so I said nothing.

Miss Francis pursed her lips, pinched out a smile, and said, "We all have our ways of coping. Me, included." Her eyes briefly darted to the ceiling. When they returned to me, she explained, "For example, one of the ways I cope with stress is blasting Taylor Swift really loud and dancing in my apartment." Shaking her head, a smile developing, she said, "I'll play the videos on YouTube and mimic her moves. I can only imagine what my downstairs neighbor thinks I'm doing when I'm jumping up and down."

Then she twisted her hips in a fast motion, as if she was literally shaking it off.

"Like I'm actually her," she said. "Me? As cool as Taylor Swift?"

Hearing this made me feel better. The fact that she was insecure as well. Looking at her with the other teachers, you would never know that she felt this way. Miss Francis was easily the coolest and hippest teacher on staff. At least, that was what I'd thought all along. I guess everyone had a surprise within them.

"Like I said, I think you're pretty cool."

She placed her palms together in prayer.

"Thanks . . . Even though you think that, I'm one of the least experienced teachers in the school. I have to prove myself every day. Prove myself to them, to my students, and to myself. Being cool will only get you so far." She swallowed. "Finding creative ways to cope is a good thing, but I think it's how far we take it. There still has to be something authentic about you. So, this is what I'm going to do for you. I'm going to let you redo your paper—"

"I don't need any pity," I interjected.

"Let me finish."

I motioned with my fingers to zip my lips and whispered, "Sorry."

"I'm going to let you redo your paper. You can still present when it's completed, but not until you talk to the counselor about what you're going through." She paused and then said, "It's okay to talk to someone. Especially after all you've gone through."

Suddenly, my body weakened and tears formed in my eyes. She had always been my favorite teacher and this gesture was one of the reasons why.

"You can't keep burying these things," she said. "Trust me. I've been there. Not with a loss or bullying, but with something else. When you bury your emotions, they'll only gnaw at you. And after a while they're going to come out."

As she talked, I slowly began to cry. A wave of emotions passed through me. This was really the first time I let my emotions get the best of me.

To lighten the mood, she said, "To quote the great poet, Taylor Swift: 'You have to shake it off.'"

Miss Francis pulled me in for a hug, and as funny as I thought her last comment was, instead of laughing, I lost it. Buckling into her, I wept. All the pain slowly exited, and when I was finally done, I felt different. I felt better. I felt confident that everything would be okay. First Lola and Ginessa, and now her.

"Is that a deal?" she asked. "Can we finally meet the real Victor?"

KISS FROM A ROSE

I hadn't spoken to Sir since the presentation. Which meant I'd texted into work twice over the last week. One more absence and I might as well find another job. But I liked this job. Make that loved this job. And more importantly, I'd grown to love Sir.

He'd texted a few times to see if I was coming in but I'd given excuses. Then, after a couple days, he'd called and left a voicemail.

"Victor," the message began. "I know you mad at me, but I need you to come down. The cart been broken into."

No way!

"Many in our block," the message continued. "They get away with money and supplies." The voicemail went on for a few more rambling seconds. Then he said, "Don't worry. No one hurt, but they steal nonetheless."

The cart was broken into? I could have been hurt. So could Sir.

I inhaled deeply and then shot him a quick text. *B there soon*

When I arrived at the food cart block, several owners were congregating in a circle. It was early Sunday morning and none of the eateries were open.

A Mediterranean fusion cart owner, Mara, was talking about needing better lighting, pointing to the nearby streetlight and how the city should put up a few more.

"I know we're responsible for our own safety," she said, scratching her temple as she addressed the small circle. "I could probably add in more lighting, but it costs money. And increased costs mean higher food prices." I could tell she was pondering the dilemma.

"You'd think that a city like Portland would have visible cameras around," another owner chimed in. "I'm sure there are cameras around, but . . ." He scanned the skies for Big Brother and then returned to the group.

Sir was standing statue still, his two hands overlapping in front of him. Very reserved and unassuming. His focus was on the cement in front of him, but he was casually nodding whenever someone spoke.

I'd always been comfortable around him but seeing him now made me nervous for some reason. My heartbeat began to race, and the last few moments of the presentation played in my head:

Victor was, uh, just trying to make joke of presentation . . . Everybody knows superheroes don't exist.

Saliva began to rise inside my throat, and I swallowed.

"Victor," called out Sir. He excused himself from the gathering and approached me.

"I got your messages," I said.

With his lips tight, he squeezed out a smile.

"Thanks for coming."

He gestured to the cart, and we entered it to have some privacy. I looked around the small area, and although the place was trashed, the feeling of being back made me smile. I'd forgotten about being nervous because I really missed this place—its smells, its appliances, its everything. My happiness was short-lived when I thought about the business being burglarized. A slight anger formed inside my gut. Every emotion possible moved through me, and I really didn't know how to act at that moment.

"I sorry about how your presentation turn out," Sir said, his vulnerability and honesty much different than the jovial ninja-chef that I'd grown accustomed to. His body language was very serious in nature. It was hard to be upset at him. Especially after what'd happened to the food cart. "But I don't think saying I a superhero was best choice."

"Then why did you do it?" I asked. "Why come?" Even though I knew I had messed up royally, Sir had every opportunity to refuse.

"You sneak attack me with video," he retaliated.

In *Superman II*, Lois Lane went out of her way to prove that Clark Kent was Superman. She was close but unsuccessful. That was until Clark's glasses fell into the fire and Lois discovered his secret. I guess my ambush was similar to this. But instead of Lois Lane, I was Lois Liar.

"I just wanted to show you the video," I explained. "That it was already out there." That wasn't the only reason, as Sir knew, dead-on, about my approach.

"You did much more than that. Paper filled with lies. Nothing about me was true." He shook his head.

"How do you know about that?" I asked. "You and Miss Francis left the room."

"When you run out, your teacher show me." His eyes widened. "It was all there. You even say my name is Benito Arguello."

My stomach sank and I felt sick.

Just then, I realized I never even knew his name. I'd been working for him for three plus months, and I always called him Sir. It didn't even cross my mind to ask. Like, wow, how douchey was I? The entire time I was preaching to him about showing his true self and I was doing the exact opposite. Everything I was doing was at his expense.

Dropping my chin, I sighed.

"Oh my God, you're right," I said. "I don't even know your name."

"It's Mark."

Mark?

"Marcus Batac," he said proudly. "But everyone call me Mark."

My shoulders dropped. I didn't really know what to say at this point. At least not about that.

"I'm really sorry about making up your life story for my own selfish reasons," I said. "But that's beside the point and why I decided to write about you. The video. The slipper. You whipped it at like five people." I was still amazed about the whole situation. "And when you threw the slipper at the mugger right before my eyes?"

"Like I say before, it was lucky."

"Both times?"

"Yes, both times."

So the video was of him!

And then, almost as if he was monologuing like the great superheroes of our time—Captain America in *Civil War* and Tony Stark in *Iron Man*—he said, "If you want to call me a hero, then fine. I was a hero at that moment. But there was nothing super about it. The truth is heroism comes from within. Like a spark. It has nothing to do with having powers. What you did was not heroic. It was the opposite. You were being a coward. I finally agree to go to teach you a lesson, but then you run out. It backfire. And I apologize for that. But then you never come back to work, and before I could talk to you, this happened. Cart get broken into."

His vision darted around the area. His whole life's work nearly taken away from him.

"Maybe this bad omen. You lie, I teach you lesson, then cart get broken into."

"I, um, I'm really sorry about all this," I said.

"It's okay," he responded. "I understand why you do it, and I sorry to hear about your parents. But as long as you learn lesson, everything fine."

"Will you forgive me?"

Nodding, he replied, "I forgive you." Then, as if he was trying to quell the tension, the hard lines of his face loosening, he said, "We don't need bad cart-ma." He giggled at his own cleverness.

Sir bowed, gesturing to me that we were back to being good again. The person I knew was starting to resurface. The one who made everyone laugh and feel happy. The one who looked at the positive in every situation. The one I looked up to as a hero. A slight smile escaped his lips. The air began to lighten, and we stood in the small kitchen area without saying a word.

"My teacher is going to let me redo my presentation," I said. Sir fidgeted uncomfortably. His face shrunk into itself. "No, no. I'm not asking you to come, if that's what you're thinking."

A sense of relief formed on his face. His shoulders, once tensed, relaxed.

"Good," he said.

"I know I've already called in a couple times," I said. "But I may need a few more days off if that's okay."

"For paper?" he asked, nodding for confirmation.

"Yeah," I answered. "I plan on writing about my boring life, and I have virtually nothing. Except some parts about my family. And I know I already have Saturday off—"

"No worries," he interjected. "I can man the truck. Once I get it back to normal." He turned to scan the area.

"I can help if you'd like," I offered. "It shouldn't take too long to get up and running again."

Together, we undid what the burglar had done, and when we got the cart back to operational again, Sir turned to me.

"For what it worth, I don't think your life is boring," he said. "You just have to find parts of life that make you happy. Then you realize you are rich."

Sir was a living fortune cookie.

We stood in silence, staring out into the abyss of downtown Portland.

Then I remembered.

"What did you want to tell me?" I asked.

"Oh yeah. We know who responsible for break-ins."

Really? Why didn't he tell me when I first got here?

He pointed out of the cart to a streetlight yards away from the block. I looked to where he was pointing. Near the top of it, affixed on a bracket, was a city camera pointing in our general direction. It was probably the same one that'd produced the juggling video that I'd found.

"Camera catch everything."

"Who was it?" I asked.

That was when Sir told me that the man responsible for the break-ins was the same mugger who had been the beneficiary of the runaway slipper from two months ago. And the same one he'd fought off. A career criminal who'd spent numerous occasions in and out of jail had stolen thousands in money and supplies from Filipino Feast and the other carts on the block.

"His name is Willie St. James," said Sir. "I will never forget his face."

"That's great news, right?" I figured that having him on camera, caught in the act, was a good thing. "Maybe the police can find him."

"May not be easy," explained Sir. "He doesn't have permanent address."

"What does that mean?"

"Police check last available address, but he not there. They say he could be anywhere. Truth is, it's nice to know his name, but we probably not get our stuff back."

From his disposition, I could tell that he was okay with that scenario. It was almost as if he'd written the loss off already. Like, as long as no one was hurt, it was okay. And then the thought hit me again. Sir only acted when someone was involved.

Outside, the other owners had returned to their respective carts to prepare for the day.

Sir then asked, "Have you eaten?"

I wasn't hungry, but I knew it was his way of showing that life went on no matter what happened. That life was how you lived it. And that life, for Filipinos, was about food.

"I could eat," I said. Nodding, he cleared some space around him on the countertop and started to make rice, pancit, and lumpia. "What all did the burglar take?"

"From what I could tell so far," he said, "they took small stash of money I use for change."

"Petty cash?"

"No, I not petty."

"No . . . never mind."

"Also get some dried goods, stuff like that." A sizzling sound rang throughout the cart. "Not too worried. Everyone okay. Just thought you should know."

"I appreciate you telling me."

"Well, you still work here, right?"

"Of course."

I looked around the cart. It was weird seeing it back to normal when, just a few minutes ago, it'd been completely disheveled. As if nothing ever happened. Like we erased it from our lives. Miss Francis letting me redo my paper felt the same. I got to pretend like my first paper never happened.

I was lost for a few moments until Sir chuckled.

"What's so funny?" I asked.

"Maybe I should get padlock for cart," he joked. "One with key. One better than door lock."

I laughed at the comment, shaking my head as he tonged some lumpia onto a plate.

"Maybe we both could carry a key around our necks," I said. "Be twins."

The stars then aligned.

"Unlock taste buds," we both said at once.

"Jinx," he shouted. We both laughed at this.

The rice cooker clicked, and shortly after, Sir was serving up a plate of food.

As I ate, I thought about what he'd said. He was right. I made up everything to make myself look good and I didn't consider him as a person. I didn't consider his feelings. I needed to.

"So, tell me about you," I said. "I want to know everything."

"Like what?"

"Like where did you come from?"

"I come from place called Metropolis," he said, then threw down a lumpia.

"Really?" I said excitedly.

He laughed.

"No," he said. He shook his head. "You really like superheroes."

I did.

"I come from small barangay in Philippines. Near the city of Pasay. Born and raised there. Then my parents and me come to States. I was around twenty-five. Don't know anyone, but they had friends in Seattle. Then after my parents passed, I met a lady." A smile brushed across his face, and I could tell he was remembering her. Searching his entire manner, I knew that she'd meant a lot to him. "We talked about getting married and having kids. I really want a son, but she died from complications. Brain cancer."

A son, which made sense why he offered me a job. He looked at me like a son. I reached out to him and patted his forearm.

"I'm sorry," I said. And I meant it.

"She's buried there, in her own spot in the cemetery," he explained. Wiping away some tears that were beginning to form, he said, "I didn't have much money to give her a good spot. But I did what I could for her."

For the most part, the headstone was bare, he told me, only her initials and her birth years spanning the small, capsule-shaped marker.

"I visited her every day at first, bringing a white rose petal and placing at base of stone," he uttered with a shrug. "I'd always kiss the rose first."

Kiss from a Rose, I thought. From *Batman Forever!*

"But after a while," he continued. "I just stopped going as much. No real reason." He sniffled, his cheeks reddening with each word uttered. "After a year or something, I went to visit, and the markings weren't readable anymore."

"The headstone decayed," I confirmed.

I hoped that wasn't the case with Mom and Dad's gravestones. I could only imagine the winter weather and its continuous rain patterns pelting the lettering so much that it caused erosion and made it difficult to read.

Sir nodded, dropping his head to his chest.

"The winter there is like here," he said. "Mostly just rain all season."

"Are your parents buried there as well?"

Sir recomposed himself. He shook his head.

"They wanted to be buried in the Philippines," he said. "Next to *their* parents." He paused for a beat. "I wish I had more time with them, done things with them. When they passed, I felt lost. Probably like how you feel." He chuckled awkwardly to himself. "They belonged to the Filipino association back home. Spent most of their time with that."

Nodding with a sigh, I said, "Yeah. I'm a member. Well, my family is. I don't really participate."

"No? I went to every event," he bragged. "The Christmas party, the meetings. Even the picnic. That's where my love of food came from."

"The picnic is coming up! That's why I needed Saturday off. I'm going."

"Yeah?"

"We always went as a family," I said. "It was the only event I went to. What about you? Going to the picnic?"

"Maybe," he said. "But I always working."

"Ginessa would be happy to see you, but she might try to recruit you."

Hearing her name must have sparked something inside him.

"Your sister cool," he said. "I like how excited she is about food. And her clothes, she the real deal." He slowly nodded. "Have her come ask me."

"I will."

My lips curled and I thought about the last time I saw my parents. Standing on the platform of the train stop, waiting for the Red Line to pick them up to take them to the airport. It was like any other time they'd visited the Philippines, and I went through the motions, believing that I would see them soon and that everything would be back to normal when they returned.

Mom hugged me tightly and Dad gave me the same lecture that he'd always given.

"Remember, you're in charge," he said. "If you need anything, your Lola's phone number is on the refrigerator."

I remembered I'd rolled my eyes. Why would I need to get in touch with Lola? Mom and Dad visited there annually. Ginessa and I never needed anything.

But he continued as if an emergency could happen.

"The Philippines is sixteen hours ahead of Portland," reminded Dad.

Afterward, the train pulled off, and I came back to the present, returning my attention to Sir.

"Can I ask you something?" I asked. "How did you pull yourself out of it? Like, from the deaths?"

"Filipinos. Members of the association reached out, offered help where they could. At first, I resisted, thinking I could do everything on my own. But they kept calling, kept coming around, kept offering help and money. Finally, I gave in. Took whatever help they offered."

His gaze looked toward the cart's window. The sun was fueling the day's spirit.

"The association helped with the costs. All the members chipped in. Some even flew with the caskets so they know it arrived."

Of course, they did. We'd received the same assistance with Mom and Dad. Man, Ginessa was right. All Filipinos were nice.

"Even though I didn't get chance to spend more time with them," said Sir, "I know they're proud of me for opening the food cart."

I looked at him, suspicious of his comment. Were they *not* proud of him? How could that be? He was awesome.

"I'm continuing our heritage through food." He cut a sharp glare at me, almost like he'd figured something out that I was unaware of. "Maybe that's what your parents want from you. To pass down heritage to next generation. To at least learn where you come from."

I thought of the family tree project, all the memories crashing down on me. The reasons for us going to the picnic each year. Continually cooking Filipino food for us to eat. Asking us to visit the Philippines with them.

"You're still young," said Sir. "But if we learn anything from our past—your parents, my parents, my lady friend—time is precious." He shrugged, his eyes cutting into mine. "Life is funny that way. What's important is you make the most of each day. Learn from your failures, listen to your loved ones and those willing to help, just try to do better."

The advice struck me harder than I expected. For a moment, it wasn't Sir lecturing me but Dad. If only I could hear his voice again.

Dad was always asking me about my life and school and even offered to meet me downtown to grab a bite to eat. Thinking about it now, he just wanted to be a part of my growing up, but I refused every time. I always had something better to do. Deep down, though, I was just embarrassed to be seen with him.

Just then, Mara, whose food cart was three down from Filipino Feast, appeared.

"Knock, knock," she said.

"Ah, kumusta," greeted Sir.

"I have some info on Willie," she said.

Instantly, my attention sparked.

"What about Willie?" I asked with great curiosity.

Mara explained that Willie was seen hanging out in Waterfront Park just off the Burnside Bridge. Apparently, he'd been doing or selling drugs and one of his meetup spots was a bench by the river.

"He's there now," she said.

"What are we going to do about it?" I asked. "We all need to get our stuff back."

"The money is probably gone," said Sir.

But he stole from us!

"Well, that's what I came over to talk to you about," Mara answered. She looked around the block, addressing the other carts with a subtle gesture and said, "I talked to some of the other owners. We kinda came up with a couple options and it seems like we're all in agreement on what to do."

The options, according to Mara, were to turn him into the police or do nothing.

"He's a criminal," she said. "Not sure what he's capable of." She shrugged. "Honestly, I've been here long enough to know this has been an ongoing problem, so shame on me for not taking the appropriate steps to protect myself and my business."

"We've got to do something," I said. "We can't just let him get away with it."

"Like Mark said, the money's probably gone," said Mara.

"That doesn't mean . . ." I started, but it didn't look like anyone was coming to my rescue.

Sir just stood quietly, slowly nodding as he stared out into the park. From where we were, the park was only three or so blocks away. Willie was legit under our noses, and nobody knew until now.

"And if he's dangerous, we probably shouldn't approach him," continued Mara. "At least, we all decided not to." She gestured to the other cart owners.

Customers began populating the block and Mara turned her head to see that a couple was reading the menu stapled next to her window.

"Anyway," said Mara. "I have customers, but I just wanted to fill you in. I don't plan on doing anything about him, so . . ." Her voice trailed off. She shrugged and then left.

When it was just the two of us, I said, "So, we're just not going to do anything?"

Sir shook his head.

"No, there is third option."

Here it was.

In my head, "Boom Boom Pow" played to a fight scene during the pilot episode of *The Legend of Sensei Tsinelas: Origin.*

I dreamed of four seasons, eight episodes per season, and thirteen Emmy Awards. Choreographed by Chef Mark, he'd go on to consult on numerous flicks starring Dave Bautista.

I rolled up my proverbial sleeves, excited about witnessing yet another instance of his superhero prowess. I was beginning to understand him. He wanted to hold his secret close—which was why he was upset about the video being posted. He kept insisting that he was lucky when he flung out the tsinelas and that superheroes didn't exist. But this was me. We just had a personal moment, and now he could trust me. He was as sly as Clark Kent keeping his identity from Lois Lane.

"Let's get our stuff back," I said.

I was anxious to get going but then Sir walked to the front of the cart, filled containers with food, and bagged them up in a plastic grocery bag.

He must need fuel before opening a can of ay nako.

He tied the handles in a pretty bow and when he was finished, he turned to me.

"Ready?"

"What's that for?" I asked.

"You'll see."

HEROISM COMES FROM WITHIN

We walked toward the park. I was getting psyched up and adrenaline started coursing through me. I swung around to look back toward the cart. Although it was back in business, the scene reminded me of what Willie had done to us.

At the intersection of Naito Parkway, the major road that separates Waterfront Park and downtown, Sir eyed the area where Willie was presumed to be.

Pointing to a park bench, Sir said, "I think that's him." His pace increased and when we got there, Sir stood in front of him.

"Willie?" The criminal stared at Sir, his eyes shifty as if he was trying to place him. "Are you Willie St. James?"

"Who's asking?"

"I'm Chef Marcus Batac," Sir said. He pointed up toward the food cart block. "I'm owner of Filipino Feast. You are responsible for thefts."

"I didn't steal nothin'," he replied defensively. He stared around like he was going to flee.

Here it was. Tsinelas time. *Boom. Boom. Pow!*

Just then, Willie bolted from the bench and took off down the riverfront.

"Ay," said Sir. "Susmaryosep!"

Sir placed the bag down and the two of us gave chase, but then Willie booked it down shore and then hopped into the river at his first chance, where it was safe enough to enter. His body fell with a splash. His head rose above the surface and it appeared like he was trying to swim. Instead, he slipped into a current and lost control.

"Help!" he screamed. "Somebody!"

There weren't a lot of people milling around, as at this time of day, most downtowners were still sleeping in.

Willie threw his head back, attempting to push the water down to try and get to the surface. There wasn't a chance as the distance was too wide. Unless he could fight the current and reach for the shore, this was a job for Chef Mar—rather, Sensei Tsinelas and Victor!

Willie screamed again.

Sir looked around the area. A skinny branch was falling to the ground from a tree that was yards away.

If only I could point my finger and pull him up with some power. Like Jean Grey and her telekinesis. I started to imagine the scenario, feeling my body beginning to levitate, but realized something. I didn't have to anymore because I was doing it. I was a superhero's sidekick!

"Hold on," Sir called out, who then moved toward Willie.

For his size, Sir moved fast, the sound of sliding tsinelas against the concrete whistling away from me.

The branch was too high up the trunk for him to reach. He looked down the river, where there was a pavilion for people to get close to the water.

"You need to get down there," he said to me. "I get branch for you to steer into water."

"How are you going to reach the branch?" I screamed.

"Don't worry," said Sir. "Just get down there!"

I looked at Willie, and the way he was fighting for his life suddenly scared me. All the confidence I'd had immediately disappeared. This wasn't just a research paper or my imagination. This was the real deal!

My hesitation was apparent, and I froze.

"Uh, I . . ."

"There's no time," Sir said. "Instinct! Use your instinct!"

Hearing that word jolted my confidence back to where it had been. Rely on instinct. The truth was I didn't have time to think. I only had time to react. I booked it toward the pavilion and slipped into the river.

Water splashed up my legs, some of it sinking into my shoes and socks. The temperature a cool fifty degrees, and suddenly, I got chills.

"Hang on!" I said to Willie, and he maneuvered toward my direction.

I tried to reach him, but with every inch I gained, my shoes became heavier, the water weighing me down. Willie just kept drifting farther and farther into the river, away from the bank. Away from civilization. Soon, he would be lost in the streams.

"Victor!" screamed Sir.

I found his voice and looked up. The branch was coming toward me. I ducked out of the way and the end of the branch fell into the river.

How did he reach that?

Then, whizzing away from the tree was a slipper. As if he'd used it to break the small limb from the trunk. The spinning slipper shrank as it moved away from me and toward Sir. Suddenly, it disappeared.

What the...?

My mind started racing. All the possibilities started going in and out of my head.

"Have him try and reach!"

Sir's voice refocused my attention to the river.

Calling out to Willie and pointing to the branch, I screamed, "Try and swim toward me!"

He did but the waves pushed him back each time. A faint cry escaped his mouth.

Moving in closer to the river, water sloshing inside my shoes around my feet, I called out again.

"You can do it! Keep your legs moving!"

The water moved higher and higher up my body the closer I got to Willie.

I guided the branch toward him, with Sir above me walking along the railing, following my lead. Once Willie was within reach, he grabbed hold of the end and Sir and I guided him back to shore.

When he was close enough, I reached out to him, pulling him back to the edge of the river where I helped him out and sat him down on a rock to catch his breath. He was scared, shocked almost, but I could tell that he was relieved to be rescued.

"Are you okay?" I asked. He nodded and then swallowed.

Sir opened the bag that he retrieved from where we'd first approached Willie. Inside were containers of pancit, adobo, lumpia, and rice.

Willie's body relaxed and he leaned in to see. His nostrils expanded; he was smelling the aroma emanating from the boxes. A second later, he closed his eyes and his lips formed a slight smile.

"This for you," said Sir. "You need more than us."

Sir offered the boxes to Willie, who stared in confusion as to what was happening.

"It's okay," said Sir.

Slowly, Willie reached out and retrieved the containers.

Sir then told me to call the police. I did, and when the cops came to take over, Sir acted as if nothing had happened. He was his cool self and I realized he was doing everything to keep the rescue quiet. Leave the glory to the police and us out of the press. But furthermore, ensure that Portland was safer.

We sat on a bench so I could wring out my socks. I wanted to say something but decided to enjoy the moment. Even though he wasn't relishing in this, I was. And it was what I needed to instill confidence within.

We then walked back to the cart.

"I wasn't expecting that," I said, referring to Willie.

"Me offer food?"

I laughed.

"No," I said. "I totally expected that. You were showing that you forgave him by offering food."

"You getting wiser," said Sir.

"I meant that I didn't expect him to try swimming across the river. Seems like people will do anything to avoid responsibility."

"What you expect then?" asked Sir.

A fight scene involving several martial artists and one large green screen played in my head. Boom microphones swirling above. Acrobatics happening around with stunt men carrying lasers attached to cables and a giant fan generating wind. We were still minutes away from the explosions.

"I guess I thought he'd fight back or just give up," I said. "That's usually what they do in superhero movies."

"Not everything happen how you envision," said Sir. "When you understand that, you make better choices."

The choreographed fight scenes in my head suddenly disappeared and I started to understand why I did the things I'd done. Like Willie, I did anything to avoid responsibility. I made my life and the lives of people around me more difficult. Then it hit me. Was I really a villain in my own world?

"You really are a superhero," I said.

"No," he dismissed quickly. "I just lucky."

"But—"

Sir raised his palm. Instantly, it silenced me.

"No more superhero talk," he said. "Heroism comes from within. We all have it. You included. That's where true power lies."

When we got back to the cart, the other owners were readying for the day. Their windows were open and signs were put up.

One cart owner had placed condiment bottles on the ledge of his window.

Mara smiled at us when she saw us.

"Looks like it's going to be a nice day," she said. "Hope business is good for you."

She was totally oblivious about what'd happened. In her mind, there were only two options.

"Same to you," said Sir. Then he looked at me. "Since you're here, want to stay and work?"

I hadn't worked in a few days, so I immediately jumped at the opportunity.

"I'd like that," I said.

We entered the cart and opened it for business. Once the window was propped open, we leaned out on the ledge and looked out into the distance.

"Chef, can I ask you something?"

"Anything," he replied.

"First, is it okay that I call you Chef?"

"That or Mark," he said. "Either fine."

"I'd prefer to call you Chef since you're my boss. And secondly, I was thinking about everything you said," I confessed. "How maybe my parents wanted to pass down their heritage to me and my sister. I was always ashamed of my culture, so I never tried learning about it." My stomach dropped at the feeling of guilt that just hit me. "Have you ever felt that way? Like have you ever resented being Filipino?"

"Not really," answered Sir. "I think people like that I'm Filipino, that's why my food so popular." His eyebrows furrowed and he took a beat, thinking about what to say next. "In fact, many people like all the different tastes. I think that why there so many Asian food carts and restaurants in Portland. Lots of different food cultures."

There were a lot of Asian themed food choices in the area. I'd never thought about that.

"To be honest," said Sir. "I just be myself. That all I could be. Seem to work out." He turned to me, placed his arm around my shoulder, and said, "I think that should be lesson in your paper. Just be Victor. And it will work out."

THE GOOD, THE BAD, THE VICTOR

I spent the next couple of days hammering out the paper. The life of Victor Dela Cruz. I wanted to include the rescue, but who would believe me now? Maybe I would someday write about it—in a different format. One that was more appropriate or suited for the topic. Somewhere I could explore my imagination.

I thought about what Sir had said. Heroism did come from within.

For research, I asked Lola and Ginessa to look through old photographs of our family with me.

"I thought you'd never ask," Lola joked. I knew that seeing pictures of Mom and Dad and us would make her day.

I also apologized for not asking sooner or taking either of their advice, but they were ready to let bygones be bygones.

I tried using the family tree as a guide, but many of those relatives were in the Philippines (specifically Dad's), and we didn't have photographic proof of them. It was a cool mystery to discover even though we couldn't match up many ancestors. Afterward, Lola taught us how to make barbecue shish kebabs. As part of my presentation, even though it wasn't a show-and-tell, I decided to bring in some Filipino food. Because deep down, I still wanted the most votes.

Miss Francis had requested that she review the revised version ahead of time. I didn't blame her. It was a way to keep me on task. To keep me truthful. To keep me from being, well, me. After she read it, she told me she was proud of me. What she said had meant a lot, considering I'd never really felt proud of myself.

Now, it was the day of the redo.

The debacle surrounding the first presentation and the talk with Sir had helped me immensely. Not to mention our saving that criminal despite him stealing from us. Again, Sir said the throw was lucky, and I wasn't certain I would ever get a real answer from him. It was frustrating, but he had his reasons, and I had to respect that.

Then it dawned on me. Getting Sir to be real with me was probably like everyone else wanting me to be real to, not only them, but myself. I finally understood. Sir was the greatest sensei ever. Everything with him was a lesson.

I was close to the classroom.

My biggest concern was how the kids, specifically Clint and Bart, would treat me after what'd happened during the first presentation. How it was made up and if they would use that to kick me when I was down.

When I arrived, Miss Francis pulled me into the hall. I'd been there so many times that there seemed to be a designated spot with my name on it. It was almost like the Hall of Justice, where each superhero had his or her own seat when they held meetings and I imagined just as much. I sat next to Superman of course!

"I'm excited for your presentation," she said. "I really like this version of your story. I knew a little about the Spanish influence on the Philippines, but it didn't really dawn on me that it was why most Filipino surnames are Spanish."

"It really didn't dawn on me either," I said. "I mean, Dela Cruz means 'of the cross.' My father, Diosdado Dela Cruz means God given of the cross or something."

"That's a pretty neat name," said Miss Francis. "It's almost superhero-esque." And then I smiled. "So, Victor Dela Cruz must mean 'victory of the cross.'" I nodded. "I imagine that would be impressive to the other students."

Voices interrupted Miss Francis and she peered into the room. No one was nearby.

"I talked to the other students, and I assure you that there will not be any interruptions."

"What did you tell them?" I asked.

"Enough for them to understand your situation." She nodded and then said, "And that I'm not going to put up with any distractions."

I took this to mean that she'd spoken to Clint and Bart, and they agreed to behave. Perhaps because of their scholarship to play football in college, or it could have been something else. I wasn't sure.

Regardless, I knew what I needed to do—tell the truth. The entire truth. All of it. The good, the bad, the Victor. And even though it wasn't filled with tales of superheroes, I was excited to give it. If only Mom and Dad could see me now.

Tapping my bag, I said, "In case they do get out of line, I brought reinforcements."

Then I unzipped it, and through the tightly wound aluminum foil, the aroma filtered out. Miss Francis inhaled, and a smile formed on her face.

"Barbecue shish kebabs," I said. Lola dropped them off a few minutes ago, so they were nice and fresh.

"They smell delicious," said Miss Francis. "You know, for all you've gone through, you've really grown as a person." I thanked her. "Now, go in there and knock this out of the park."

I powered through the presentation, only stammering across a few words as I read the paper verbatim. For the most part, the kids were respectful. There weren't any snide or smart-alecky comments. At least none that crept into my brain. It was as if time had reversed, and it never actually happened.

When I got to the final paragraph, I felt at peace. A feeling of relief released from my body and into the universe.

"In conclusion, I'd spent half of my life living as a Filipino-American teenager. My whole existence revolved around white culture. I don't speak with an accent; rather, the only difference between me and most of you is the color of my skin. Oh, and that my name literally means victory of the cross."

I heard Miss Francis laugh behind me, and my confidence increased. I continued.

"I'm essentially a white, brown kid, and it was enough for me to be ashamed of my race. My parents passed away in a plane crash last year, and they never got the chance to see me fully embrace my culture. This is my biggest regret. And it's what I plan on spending the rest of my life doing—learning about my family, my culture, and myself." I closed my eyes and exhaled. "Thank you."

The class instantly applauded. Hearing the reaction, I stole a look to the class but, most importantly, to Miss Francis. She quickly shook her hips like Taylor Swift, and I laughed.

"Great job, Victor!" Madelyn piped.

Timothy agreed by shouting, "Way to go!"

I relished in the moment, but then Miss Francis settled down the class.

"Victor," she said. "Before you sit down, in your presentation, you mention that you plan on learning about your culture and your family. How do you plan on doing that?"

"I was thinking about taking that trip to the Philippines," I said. "It'll be good for me and my sister to go. Plus, my grandmother may not have another opportunity."

Miss Francis smiled.

"I think that's a great idea."

"Oh, I almost forgot," I said. "I brought in some kebabs to try. Unfortunately, I only have some for a few of you." I pulled the tray out of my bag. The smell immediately escaped into the class, and the kids closest to me perked up. I passed them out to Timothy and Madelyn and then spread the rest of them out. I was just happy that I got a second chance and that my grade would reflect my effort. I would graduate from high school with my GPA intact. That was all that mattered to my parents, and frankly, that was all that mattered to me.

After class, I was filling Ginessa in on the presentation.

"I'm very proud of you," she said. "I know it's difficult to talk about Mom and Dad, but it really helped me work through my emotions." She wrapped her arm around my waist and leaned into me. "It took a lot of guts to do that in front of the class. Especially in front of—"

As we exited the school, Clint and Bart were crowding the entrance. Standing around them like supervillains from the Legion of Doom were the rest of the football players.

"Are you still coming over?" Clint asked Ginessa. He then gestured to Bart with his thumb. "We need help with our projects, too. Since Victor gave such a great presentation."

"I'm sorry, but I can't tonight," she said.

Ginessa had told me earlier about her plan to perfect the flan, once and for all. Seeing her even consider dropping something she truly looked forward to for Clint and Bart nearly made me ill.

"Maybe . . . " Then she stopped and tapped her finger on her chin. As if she was actually considering this.

"Well, tonight works best for us," said Clint. His voice subtly became stern and forceful, like he was almost demanding her to come.

Ginessa cut me a glance, and her usually confident demeanor seemed fragile. Like here was my moment, and I didn't want to let her down. Again. Slowly, she shook her head.

Instantly, as if my inner Bruce Banner was two thirds transformed into The Hulk, my hands closed into clenched fists, and I said, "She said she couldn't tonight!"

"She can answer for herself," said Clint.

I knew that he had to maintain his cool guy persona, especially in front of the growing crowd, so this attitude didn't surprise me. I prepared myself, the tightness in my fists traversing up my arms and into my torso. Suddenly, all the fear evaporated from me. Who did this guy think he was?

"She said," I repeated firmly, my heartbeat steady, my jaw set, and my gaze piercing into Clint's soul, "she can't tonight. She has other things to do that're more important." I stepped closer to Clint, my head slightly tipping back to address him. "Okay?"

"Victor," said Ginessa, attempting to pull me back with her hand. But I wasn't listening.

Clint's brows furrowed and his eyes narrowed, and for the next few moments, we stood like sculptures holding our ground.

At this point, I wasn't sure what had come over me, but I was tired of being pushed around. I was tired of not being there for Ginessa. And this was my chance to make it up to her.

"It's all right," said Ginessa. "Really."

"No, it's not," I replied. Then, to Clint, I said, "In fact, it wasn't okay for her to help you in the first place." My heart pounding to the heavy beat of "Boom Boom Pow," I said, "Why can't you do your own homework?"

Unbeknownst to me, the crowd around us had multiplied. Clint exhaled heavily, his warm breath hitting my face, and I wondered what I had gotten myself into. But I stayed strong.

"Don't make me angry," I said. "You wouldn't like me when I'm angry."

Clint and Bart looked at each other. I was holding my breath for what seemed like hours, and I braced myself for the worst. But nothing happened. Instead, Bart elbowed Clint, which must have dispelled his trance. Clint's demeanor softened.

Clint scanned the eyes of those around us and said, "We probably have enough material to finish on our own." His gaze then drifted over to me. "Look. I'm sorry that you went through all that. With your parents and all."

An apology?

Bart displayed a pointed smile.

"Thank you for all your help," he said to Ginessa. "Just let us know if you're available." He then turned to me and nodded. "Great presentation."

Clint walked away, and slowly, the crowd dispersed and Ginessa and I were left standing by ourselves. Just like that, the thickness of the air dissipated.

"Don't make you angry?" said Ginessa playfully. "Oh, Victor."

LIKE A SUPERHERO AND VILLAIN

On the train ride home, I sat across from Ginessa. Today's baro't saya was charcoal gray colored. The dress was slender fit across her upper torso and fanned out around her knees. She almost looked like a futuristic protagonist who returned to the past to save the world.

And maybe she was.

Her backpack rested on her lap. The zipper wasn't completely zipped closed. The notebook's corner peeked out of the bag.

The train bounced along a rough patch, which forced the zipper to open, and the notebook slipped out.

My gaze found the notebook. The infamous notebook. Although the encounter with Clint and Bart was over, the adrenaline of my victory was still flowing through me.

Ginessa slid it back into her bag. She zipped it closed.

"I guess you don't have to help Clint with his homework anymore."

She shrugged and then said, "I know, but I probably still will.

"I'm sure," I replied. "You're a good person." Then, after a short pause, I said, "Can I ask you something?"

"Sure."

"How did you even connect with him?" A first-year student and the king of the school seemed like an unlikely combination.

"I overheard him and Bart talking about it in the hallway," she explained. "How numerous teachers had informed the football coach about their grades." She shrugged, like it was nothing. "One of the nice things about keeping to yourself is that you're invisible to most people. Especially the popular kids."

Her superpower was invisibility.

"When I approached him, of course, he was his typical cool guy self. No big deal, none of my business, etcetera. I told him that it wasn't my scholarship to lose. This seemed to trigger him.

As I started to walk away, he called out to me." A winning smile escaped her lips, and she said, "That's when I saw Clint was actually concerned. You could tell. Just in his voice. It wasn't the same Clint anymore."

"You mean he wasn't a villain?" I chuckled.

Shaking her head, she said, "Not at all. It was like he was really scared to fail." Her shoulders raised. I could tell she was loving every second of this. "And why wouldn't he be?"

"So, he does have feelings."

The train stopped by the university, and several people entered and exited. I smiled at a woman walking by, and then I returned to Ginessa.

"Honestly, seeing how they treated you was the basis for me helping them," she confessed. "But the more I got to know them, the more I realized they weren't any different than us. They're typical teenagers trying to please their parents as well."

A thought occurred to me.

"I thought their families were loaded though," I said. "Car dealership? Chocolate company?"

"I can't really speak for Bart's family," she began, "but he did mention a couple times that he didn't have time to do his homework because he had to work at the shop." My lips pursed, and I nodded. "Just because your family owns a business, it doesn't mean you're rich. He was going to school, playing football, then working part-time for his parents."

All of this was news to me. I'd only seen them in class and around the school. The image they portrayed to us underlings. I guessed it was no different than the image I was trying to portray. In that respect, we were all the same.

"Clint, though?" she said. "He needs this scholarship to get into college because the car dealership has been failing, and I guess the money situation isn't as good as he makes it out to be." A slight smirk escaped the side of her mouth. "To be honest, he doesn't have the stature to play football professionally. Once he realizes that, he's going to have to work like everyone else. It's almost like I was his last hope."

"Wow," I said, impressed by her assessment. "Maybe his life isn't so great, after all."

"I agree."

"If he has so many problems, why take it out on me?"

"Duh," she said. "Think about it like a superhero and villain. He's insecure about his intelligence so his superpower comes from bullying people like you. Smart people. The family tree project exposed your weakness, and he used it against you to work through his own insecurities. It's probably why it seemed so personal. To keep his power, he had to torture the nerds. With you being the number one nerd. In his mind, at least."

"Thanks," I said, chuckling.

"What? It's okay to be a nerd," said Ginessa. "I'm a nerd. Look at how I dress. Look at my interests. I'm a freshman. I shouldn't be dressing like this. In his mind, I should be worshipping the ground he walks on."

At that moment, I almost felt bad for Clint and Bart. All the pressure they had playing football. It wasn't just about being popular; instead, they needed a way to get into college. High school was just as challenging for them.

This revelation lightened my mood. I wanted to look at the bright side of things.

"Don't take this the wrong way but I actually think you and Clint have a lot in common," said Ginessa. "I mean, Clint's ringtone is the 'Imperial March.' One day, it went off like a thousand times." She shrugged. "And then another time, they asked if I could bring some egg rolls for them."

I laughed, thinking about Sir's lumpia and egg roll drug ring.

"You're not actually suggesting I befriend them, are you?"

"Oh, not at all. I don't think he'd ever sink that low. Befriending his number one enemy? Right. I'm just saying." She dismissed this idea so quickly her face blurred. "And I didn't bring egg rolls to them," she said. "There was no way I was going to feed them after how they treated you. Filipinos use food to bring people together. And I wasn't about ready to do that."

Hearing that gave me relief, and I felt the same way. It wasn't a coincidence that I'd only brought enough for a few of the kids.

The computerized voice above us announced the next stop. Pioneer Square. I pointed up to indicate our departure, and then I began to gather my belongings.

"I'd never seen how disappointed they were when I refused to bring them food," she said. "I literally could have made them do anything for me at that point." We both laughed. Ginessa laughed even harder, her round cheeks rising high on her face.

I looked at Ginessa and thought, *This was her world and I just lived in it.* She was like Professor X. Some mutant leader whose power was out of this world.

The doors opened, and we stepped off the train.

"Want to make a pit stop first?" I asked. Ginessa's brows furrowed. She was intrigued. "I want to stop by my work. I was talking to Chef about the picnic, and he said he'd go if you ask him in person."

"Great!" she said. "He was a lot of fun. I can see why you like working there." Then she patted me on the shoulder, almost as if she was proud of me. "You two make a great team."

SMOOTH, CHEF, SMOOTH

The Saturday of the picnic was sunny and warm, a perfect temperature for the Filipino-American gathering. Area members and their families came out to enjoy good food, good company, dancing, karaoke, and the presence of the newest association member, Chef Mark Batac, who received an ovation.

Thanks to Ginessa, he'd graciously accepted the invitation and paid dues for the next decade. Then he yelled, "No paybacks!" even though it didn't make any sense. I knew that he just wanted to enjoy life as it came, having fun in the process.

Many people recognized him from his food cart, and those who didn't, quickly became familiar when Ginessa introduced him, bragging about Filipino Feast and how popular it was.

Sir put his hands together in prayer when Ginessa finished welcoming him and then meandered around the park to check out the festivities.

Random balloons were tied to the gazebo's posts and welcome signs and banners strategically placed so that members knew where the party was.

As if it was difficult not to know. Filipinos had the knack of being noticed, their loud, energetic voices and deep laughter harassing everyone who walked by, asking if they were hungry or not. They were just traits of Filipinos. Something to fully accept or be ashamed of. For years, I'd spent time being ashamed. Now I was going to accept them. Completely.

Two teenagers were dancing Tinikling, a Filipino dance that involved people tapping and sliding hollow bamboo sticks on two-by-fours while participants danced in between them, stepping in and out and around the sticks as they slid together.

Tinikling was the national dance of the Philippines, and I wanted nothing more than to be at the Filipino-American picnic experiencing it. I looked at Lola, and then to Ginessa, and smiled. Being here with family really touched my soul. It felt perfect. I wished that Mom and Dad were here with us.

Choreographed to a tee, the dance routine dazzled onlookers, bringing Filipino culture to the forefront and to those driving by the public park. Some passersby stopped their cars to get out and watch, while others honked in appreciation.

As I enjoyed the dancing, Ginessa worked a booth nearby with another member, taking in donations to keep the association alive. I watched her converse with members, her enthusiasm apparent with each word spoken. I could tell that she loved being a part of this group, like there wasn't a care in her mind if anyone knew it. She would make a great president one day, and I was anxious to be a part of the association when she was.

Sir sidled next to me, interrupting the moment.

"Nice outfit," he said, scanning my attire.

I was wearing a barong. Dad had gotten me one years ago, and he always wanted me to wear one to Filipino events like he used to, but I never did.

"Thanks," I said. "I've had it for a while, but this is the first time I actually wore it."

"Looks good on you," said Sir. "Make statement."

"I'm glad you came."

"Remind me of association back home," he said gleefully, taking in the atmosphere. "Bring back lots of memories."

Lola appeared. She was dressed up more than usual—a summer dress with sandals—and was wearing makeup. It was my first time I'd seen her all done up like this. She reached her hand out to Sir, who took it.

"We haven't formally met," she said, her eyelashes batting wildly.

OMG, was she flirting? She was much older than Sir, but I totally understood. He was magnetic.

"Yes," said Sir. "You're Victor's auntie?" He smiled nervously.

Smooth, Chef, smooth, I thought, rolling my eyes away from me.

Lola squealed in delight at the comment. I could sense that she was floating on air.

"Would you like to get some food?" she asked. "Enjoy the activities?"

He accepted, and the two disappeared in the mix of attendees.

Clapping startled me a bit, and when I looked, I saw that Tinikling had ended, and everyone had dispersed from the area for other events to get lost in.

Ginessa came up next to me, bumping my shoulder with hers.

"I'm glad you're here," she said.

"I am too."

"I know I keep saying this but I'm really proud of you," she said. "You've really stepped up. And I know we cleared things up a little bit, but I just wanted to say one thing."

"Okay," I said. "What's on your mind?"

"When Mom and Dad passed, I expected you to take care of me. Take care of us. But you didn't come through. You only thought about yourself. I had to turn to my friends to help me work through my feelings because I felt alone." I raised my finger to interject, but she shushed me. "Please let me finish." I pinched my lips and then nodded. "Since you weren't there, I had to step up and be the adult in the family. I know we have Lola but she's not going to be around much longer. And I'm still a kid, I just thought—"

"You don't have to explain," I said, interrupting her. She looked uncomfortable at first, but then she sighed. "Really." I became silent, thinking about all that I'd put Ginessa through. "You're one hundred percent right. You are a kid, and you're allowed to be a kid. I'm sorry for taking that away from you." Looking around us, I said, "Even though you did all this." I gestured out to the picnic's attendees.

The park was packed with members from the Portland area and beyond.

She smiled, then leaned into me and hugged me. We shared a quiet moment together, both lost in our thoughts.

"Good turnout," she then uttered, scanning the entire park in one swoop.

"It is," I said. "You did a great job putting this together."

"It wasn't all me," she replied. "But thank you."

An awkward silence.

I pointed to her outfit with my lips. Ginessa was wearing the most extravagant baro't saya I'd ever seen. You would think she stood out but most people at the picnic were decked out in Filipino wear. Barong shirts, fancy Capiz-shelled jewelry, you name it.

"I love that dress," I said.

"It was Mom's," she answered. "It's a perfect fit."

Chatter and laughter filled the space around us. Some people were louder than others. The smell of food tickled my nose, and I sat amazed at how many people were in attendance. How many Filipinos were here enjoying themselves, not caring about the Clints and Barts of the world? Instead, they were all just having fun, being themselves. Being true to who they were. Being Filipino.

I turned to her and smiled.

"Mom and Dad would be proud of you."

Then I looked up to the heavens and thanked them for a pleasant day. It couldn't have been more perfect.

Ginessa grazed my forearm.

"They'd be proud of you, too," she said.

Just then, a teenager walked by with a plate of Ginessa's flan. He took a quick bite, peering around for his friends, and then stopped short to inspect the dessert. His face brightened, his eyes widening. He swallowed down another spoonful then licked his lips.

"Looks like your flan is a hit."

"It came out perfect."

"Hey," I said. "I almost forgot. I want to show you something." I whipped out my phone and pulled up an article I discovered from *Esquire Philippines*. "Once I found out Chef's real name, I started researching it."

The article was titled "Alleged Superhero Disappears from Philippines."

The article went on to say that an alleged tsinelas-wielding superhero who worked with activists during the failed impeachment of then President Joseph Estrada suddenly vanished from the Philippines in 2000.

"It referenced a guy they just called Batak with a 'K' and not a 'C,'" I said. "According to the internet, Batac with a 'C' means 'the people's pooling their efforts together.'"

"So, you think it's him?" asked Ginessa.

"Maybe," I said. "Think about it. He worked with activists . . . and his name means 'the people's pooling their efforts together.' I wonder if all these so-called efforts made him flee the Philippines. When we finally had a heart to heart, he told me he came to the States when he was like twenty-five. The timeline makes sense. If this is true, talk about the most incredible origin story ever!"

We looked at Sir, who was having a blast with Lola.

"I don't even know what to think," said Ginessa. "Are you at least going to ask him about it?"

"I think I'm going to write a paper," I quipped.

She elbowed me. Hard.

"Victor?"

"I'm just kidding," I said, laughing at my own joke. "I'm not. It's obvious he wanted to keep it a secret."

"If it's even him," she replied. I snickered. "And if superheroes exist."

I was ready to die on this hill, but before I could respond, a beat suddenly erupted from the karaoke machine, surprising both Ginessa and me.

My body lifted. It was "Boom Boom Pow," our fictitious superhero theme song.

Looking up at the karaoke station, I saw Sir holding the microphone. But how did he know? I never told him about it.

He was twirling the cord like a lasso, showing off his skills. A smitten Lola was ogling over him, standing just in front of the makeshift stage.

Sir took her hand and pulled her close to him. They stood side-by-side.

"Victor," his voice rang thru the speakers. "Ginessa. Come up here."

As the beat continued to play around us, Sir and Lola sang the lyrics.

Ginessa ran to the stage in apparent excitement. I followed. And when we positioned ourselves—Me, Ginessa, Lola, and Sir —the four of us looked like a watered-down version of the Black Eyed Peas. A roster that couldn't get a record deal if we tried.

But I didn't care. Instead, I joined in.

The song played on, with each of us fumbling over the lyrics. It was funny that I'd heard this song a thousand times, but I didn't know the actual words. So I just made them up as I sang along.

♪ I'm always Filipino late . . . Look at all the lumpia I ate . . . ♪

Ginessa chuckled at this line, which made me burst out laughing. Eventually, the four of us were buckled over in hysteria. The song continued without words.

I wasn't sure what people thought about us. Only that the people in attendance were cheering us on. Joining in on the laughter. One kid started breakdancing, as every Filipino-American association had that one kid who could win a breakdance battle if their life depended on it.

People continued to enjoy themselves, pointing at us, possibly thinking, "Black Eyed Peas? More like Black Eyed Please!" because I didn't know how bad we sounded. I just knew we were bad!

And you know what? I didn't care.

When the song ended, Ginessa stayed back and announced the upcoming balloon throwing challenge. She rambled through the instructions and talked about the prizes that the association was giving out.

"So, grab a partner," she said excitedly. "Then meet out in the grass by the balloons."

Simultaneously, Lola and Sir pointed at each other. Sir kicked off his slippers. Lola slipped off her sandals and then she grabbed his hand and pulled him toward the line of water balloons just a few yards from the stage.

I waited for Ginessa to leave the stage so I could be her partner. I walked over to join the activity, but I tripped over one of Sir's tsinelas.

I looked down at the slipper and it sparkled.

My heart skipped a beat.

Picking it up, I tossed it, and it was then that I saw the magic before my eyes, as it propelled forward in a smooth rotation and then returned to me.

"Victor?" called out Ginessa. "Ready?"

I stood frozen, and my eyes darted over toward Sir, who saw the entire thing.

Then he put his fingers to his lips, and with a wink, he mouthed, "Shh."

ACKNOWLEDGEMENTS

I didn't know that I wanted to write this story until I did.

Forty or so years ago, I had an obsession with superheroes. To be honest, I still do. It's not as bad as it was back then, though. At least I'm not walking around the house with a beach towel pinned around my neck like a cape. Or attempting to lift the end of the couch with my brothers sitting on it. "Seriously," I would say. "Just sit on the end near me and watch me lift it up over my head."

That's because each Saturday I would wake up super early to watch "Super Friends." Superman was my favorite. Everything about him was super. His powers, his backstory, everything. His backstory—thinking about it as a brown-skinned white kid in the Midwest—was the best immigrant story ever. Some alien from another planet who appeared on a Midwestern farm and became loved and revered when he wore tights and a cape. But he only got that attention as Superman and not as Clark Kent. Ergo, my dilemma: How would I be loved and revered like Superman when I was only mild-mannered Jason Tanamor whose kryptonite was cultural identity? Could it be as simple as wearing tights and a cape?

This was the precise moment when I dreamt up a story about a kid struggling with cultural identity who was obsessed with superheroes. But it was only an idea, and nothing more. How would I actually write it? And what type of "superhero" would I write about? I wasn't the writer Jerry Siegel, the creator of Superman, was. I wasn't even Clark Kent at this point. He was at least a reporter for the Daily Planet. Both had so much more experience. I couldn't write anything. Nothing about me screamed "write." Hell, I wasn't even right-handed.

But then, something happened. I was a typical butthead son to my father.

I credit him for inadvertently creating Sensei Tsinelas. When my brothers and I were kids, my father used to threaten to spank us with one of his tsinelas. Don't get me wrong, we all deserved it. All he had to do was slide the slipper off his foot and raise it above his head. From there, we disappeared as fast as we could, never to witness the aftermath. Oftentimes, I would peek out from where I was hiding, only to see him returning the slipper to his foot while laughing in the process.

So, it got me thinking... Wouldn't it be awesome if my father could stop crimes as they happened by whipping out his slipper at them? And what if the slipper was like a boomerang in that it would release from his hand, knock out the criminal, and then boomerang back to him? I mean, it worked on us. Not the crimes part, but it definitely kept us from causing trouble. This newly-created superhero stayed in my head until this book.

But what about his secret identity? What would that look like? I know! Base Sir on my father!

A lot of Sir's personality comes from my father. Both are quirky, animated, and only have one mission—to feed people. The question "Have you eaten?" that Sir always asks Victor is the first thing my father asks me every time I see him. So it was natural to make Sir a Filipino chef.

Finally, a superhero was born.

Now to the writing part of the story. There are a lot of people I want to thank.

A huge thanks goes to Luis Ramos, who served as the project manager for my last book, *Love, Dance & Egg Rolls*. We've since become friends, and when he asked me if I was working on anything new, I told him about Sensei Tsinelas. It was only in a dirty draft form and had an outrageous storyline and even more ridiculous ending. He was excited to read it, nonetheless, for nothing more than his love for superhero stories and books in general. When he finished, he provided detailed notes on the story, almost like he was "working" on it in a professional capacity. I couldn't believe the level of consideration he provided for my story, and it would not be here if it weren't for him.

To my forever "editor" Bonnie, who not only puts up with me in a marital capacity, but also as a reader. She is responsible for making this story more realistic and less . . . Jason. She will always tell me like it is, and I can't thank her enough for it.

To Robyn at Ooligan Press, who, during the Portland Book Festival in November 2022, asked if I had anything in the works. The book was only a couple drafts in, and by her asking, it forced me to dedicate the next few months to it. So, thank you for that!

To all the editors at Ooligan Press who worked on it. If you spent one second on this manuscript to make it better and more readable, this book is as much yours as it is mine.

And to writer Jerry Siegel and artist Joe Shuster for creating Superman; you two are the reason why I became obsessed with superheroes.

ABOUT THE AUTHOR

Jason Tanamor is a Filipino American writer and author. Named as one of the "5 Best Modern Filipino Writers" by *Pinas Global Newspaper* and listed as one of *Positively Filipino*'s "Fil-Ams Among the Remarkable and Famous," Tanamor is the acclaimed author of the Filipino-themed novels *Vampires of Portlandia, Love, Dance & Egg Rolls*, and *The Legend of Sensei Tsinelas*. He was nominated for the 2024 UCLA Allegra Johnson Writing Prize and he has been featured in several Filipino publications like *Esquire Philippines, CNN Philippines, Philippine Daily Inquirer,* and *Asian Journal*. Tanamor currently lives and works in Illinois.

LAND ACKNOWLEDGEMENT

We acknowledge and honor Indigenous communities—past, present, and future—whose land we currently reside on here at Portland State University. This includes the traditional and ancestral homelands of the Multnomah, Wasco, Cowlitz, Kathlamet, Clackamas, Bands of the Chinook, the Tualatin Kalapuya (Atfalati), Molalla, and many other Indigenous nations who made their homes along the Wimahl, Nch'i-Wàna, or swah'netk'qhu (all meaning "Big River or "Great River"), also known by its colonized name, the Columbia River. Descendants of these tribes are primarily members of the Confederated Tribes of Grand Ronde, Confederated Tribes of Siletz Indians, and the Chinook Nation. We acknowledge the current and long-standing oppression faced by Indigenous peoples and recognize that we are here because of the sacrifices forced upon them. We encourage everyone to find ways to support and connect with Indigenous communities and the land itself, and to remain committed to their justice and liberation. We also encourage folks to read the PSU Conflict Resolution department's Land Conflict Acknowledgement for further learning about the history of land conflict in this geographical area.

We attribute the name of our press to native peoples in Oregon. The Ooligan (also spelled Ourigan, Eulachon, or the Saak by the Tlingit peoples) is a Chinook word for a small candlefish that is abundant in the Pacific Northwest. The nutrient-rich oil produced from boiling the fish was traded between coastal and inland First Nations all along the Pacific coast, from California to Alaska, bringing prosperity and health to native communities. These routes were known as grease trails. Gradually, the L in Ooligan was replaced with an R, giving us the sound "ooregon". This usage became the name of a place and assumed its current spelling of Oregon in the course of history. We would like to honor David G. Lewis for his contributions to the press, along with his writings in the co-authored article Ourigan: Wealth of the Northwest Coast, which informed the name of our press in 2001.

We acknowledge the lack of Indigenous and people of color representation throughout the publishing industry, both in professional positions and as authors. Our press strives to publish culturally relevant titles from our local, diverse voices in order to make literature accessible and redefine who has a place within its pages. We commit to actively creating space for and uplifting Indigenous and other diverse authors through our work, including our How To: Publishing workshop and continued community partnerships.

Ooligan Press

Ooligan Press is a student-run publishing house rooted in the rich literary culture of the Pacific Northwest. Founded in 2001 as part of Portland State University's Department of English, Ooligan is dedicated to the art and craft of publishing. Students pursuing master's degrees in book publishing staff the press in an apprenticeship program under the guidance of a core faculty of publishing professionals.

Project Managers
Annie Egghart
Janeth Hernandez

Acquisitions
Becca Moss
Rin Kane
Angela Griffin
Emmily Tomulet

Pitch Prep
Amber Finnegan
Anna Wehmeier Giol
Noraa Gunn
Isabel Kristensen
Cecilia Too
Jennifer Wurtele

Editorial
Jessica Pelton
Marissa Muraoka
Jordan Bernard
Tanner Croom

Design
Ariana Espinoza
Marielle LeFave
Laura Renckens

Digital
Kari Olson
Madelynn Sare
Cecilia Too
Mara Palmieri

Marketing & Publicity
Rory Miner
Yomari Lobo

Online Content & DEI
AJ Adler
Jules Luck

Operations
Kara Herrera
Haley Young

Book Production
Rori Anderson
DJ Borden
Araliya Dooldeniya
Elle Edwards
Amber Finnegan
Mads Forsythe
Noraa Gunn
Eden Herzog
Julie Kanta
Grace King
Marielle LeFave
Dylan McDonald
Becca Moss
Quentin Nall
Peter Ngunga
Mara Palmieri
Jessica Pelton
Tidari Pizana
Abby Relph
Madelynn Sare
Annaliese Smith
Coriander Smith